Tales from the Canyons of the Damned Ominibus 10

PRESENTED BY USA TODAY BESTSELLING AUTHOR

DANIEL ARTHUR SMITH

This book is a work of fiction and any resemblance to persons, living or dead, is purely coincidental. Tales from the Canyons of the Damned All rights reserved Holt Smith ltd Collection Copyright © 2019 by Daniel Arthur Smith

Superclasico by Gustavo Bondoni. Copyright © 2018 Gustavo Bondoni. Used by permission of the author.

The Fourth by M. M. De Voe. Copyright © 2018 M. M. De Voe. Used by permission of the author.

Killer Shot by Ann Stolinsky. Copyright © 2018 Ann Stolinsky. Used by permission of the author.

Hide and Seek by Daniel Arthur Smith. Copyright © 2019 Daniel Arthur Smith. Used by permission of the author.

Auntie_lena314 by Molly Thynes. Copyright © 2018 Molly Thynes. Used by permission of the author.

A Wonder Made of Skulls by Barry Charman. Copyright © 2018 Barry Charman. Used by permission of the author.

Masks by Jason LaVelle. Copyright © 2018 Jason LaVelle. Used by permission of the author.

Off-World Kick Murder Squad VI by Daniel Arthur Smith. Copyright © 2019 Daniel Arthur Smith. Used by permission of the author.

Exclusionary Symbiosis by Nathan M. Beauchamp. Copyright © 2019 Nathan M. Beauchamp. Used by permission of the author.

Ship of the Dead by Charles Barouch. Copyright © 2019 Charles Barouch. Used by permission of the author.

Last Visit to the Park by Terry R. Hill. Copyright © 2019 Terry R. Hill. Used by permission of the author.

Off-World Kick Murder Squad VII by Daniel Arthur Smith. Copyright © 2019 Daniel Arthur Smith. Used by permission of the author.

Special thanks to Jessica West
Cover Design By Daniel Arthur Smith

 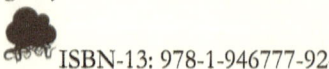 ISBN-13: 978-1-946777-92-8

For Susan, Tristan, & Oliver, as all things are.

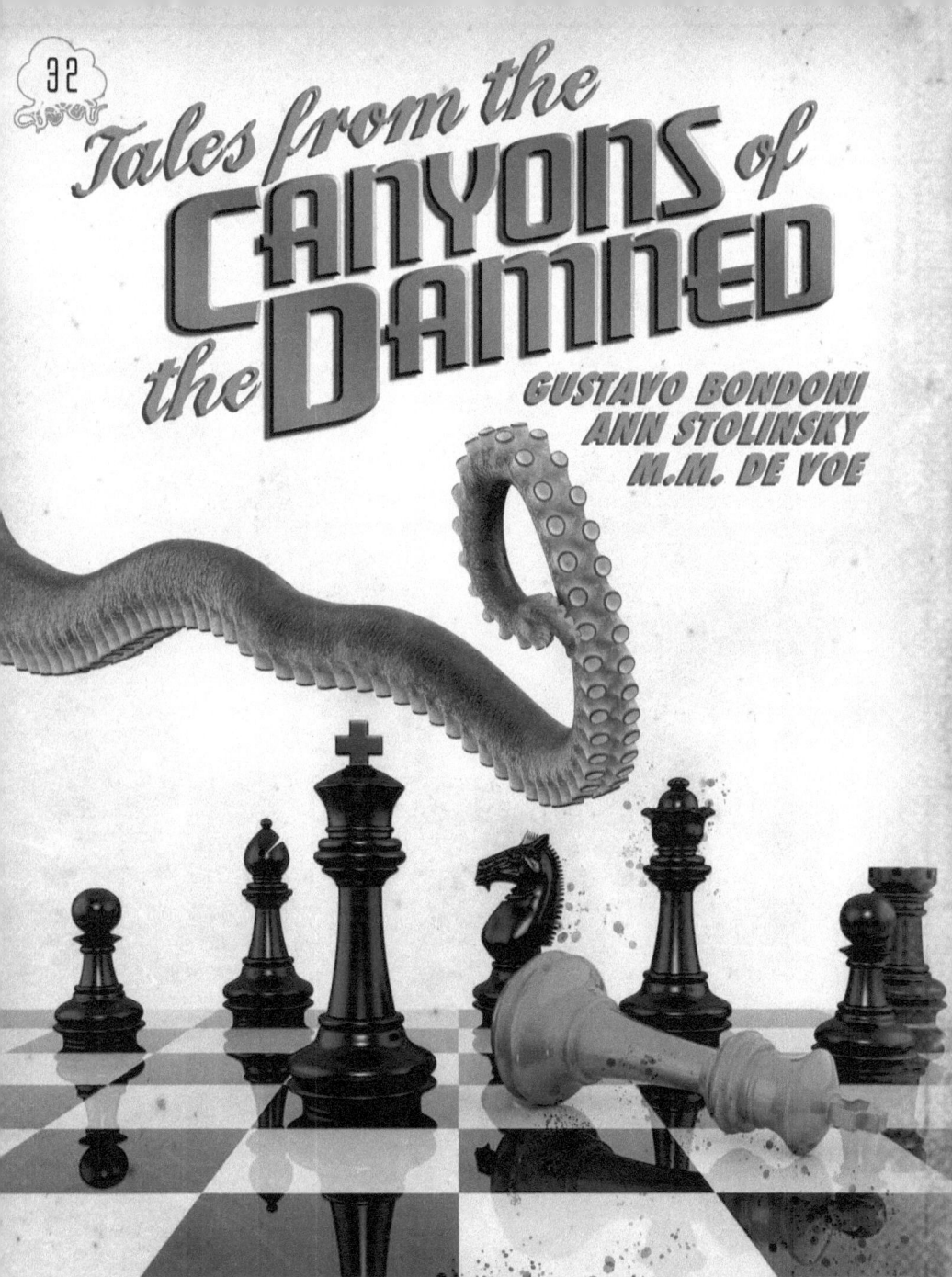

32

Tales from the CANYONS of the DAMNED

GUSTAVO BONDONI
ANN STOLINSKY
M.M. DE VOE

PRESENTED BY USA TODAY BESTSELLING AUTHOR
DANIEL ARTHUR SMITH

Superclasico
Gustavo Bondoni

THEIR PROTECTIVE COLORATION kept them safe. Yellow and blue were more powerful than any other talisman in this particular slum, no matter how much it chafed to have to wear the colors of the Boca Juniors club. Well, they could always bathe afterwards.

"Man, and I thought our place smelled," Dario whispered, wrinkling his nose.

"You know what they say about the *bosteros*," Emilio replied, referring to the fans of their hated rivals. But he kept his voice down. Even with the right colors, they were strangers there and therefore objects of scrutiny. Keeping their voices down would give their audience one less thing to analyze.

Of course, most of the eyes that followed their progress belonged to people whose curiosity was had been nearly extinguished by the noxious poverty and aimless drudgery of their daily lives. The great majority of people would forget them as soon as they passed—grateful that the strangers hadn't brought violence with them.

"I always thought that was just something we said to put them down."

"Everything people say has some truth to it."

The shantytown seemed to go on for miles. Muddy paths wound between shacks built from that combination of corrugated metal and cardboard that immediately told you that you were in one of the poorest sections of the Third World. And Dario was right. It *did* smell.

1

"Over there," Emilio said, pointing to one of the few concrete structures in the maze: an abandoned control tower that loomed over the shacks beside it and was the only hint that the place they were walking in had once been a railroad yard...before the poor had overrun it. The tracks had been sold for scrap long ago.

Though it looked close at hand, it took them nearly ten minutes to reach the building. There was only one path that led to the door, and it wound in a spiral around the building a few times, meandering this way and that between the shacks before finally reaching the dark entrance which gaped at them. It had once held a double door, but now stood empty.

Dario and Emilio stopped some thirty feet from the door—where the last curve in the path had led them. "We're going to have a hell of a time getting out again," Dario said.

"Not if we do this right. No noise. If there are other people in there, we just walk away."

"They say she works alone. Other people throw off her magic."

"They say a lot of things," Emilio replied. "I don't even believe she has any magic."

"Then why are you even here?"

"Because the rest of you believe it. Because if I didn't come, someone else would be here in my place, and I'd lose the respect of the *barra*."

"How can you not believe? They've won ten games in a row. They're terrible, but they never lose. It has to be magic."

"I don't believe in that stuff. And besides, we haven't played them yet. The Superclasico is in Monumental Stadium this year. They can never win there." It was true. Boca hadn't won the game between Argentina's two most popular sides on River Plate's home field in years.

"Whatever. Just in case, I have my *gualicho* with me," Dario replied.

Emilio grunted. If that ugly thing made of bones and feathers made the man feel safe, he wouldn't talk it down. The last thing he wanted was for his companion to lose his nerve. "Let's go inside."

"I don't like it. Shouldn't there be guards here if she's so important?"

"I already told you. The woman needs to work alone."

The dim interior seemed pitch dark to eyes accustomed to the sunlight. They stood just inside the threshold, waiting for their vision to adjust. When it did, they saw a cavernous square room lit by a single bare bulb in the center.

Seated on the floor right beneath the bulb was a woman with her back to them. There were a number of items arrayed in front of her: papers, photos, sports shirts and what, in the dim light, looked like the carcass of some rodent. To judge by her long, bedraggled blond hair and slim body, she was much younger than Emilio had expected

The woman was jerking violently, twitching like someone having a seizure. At one point, she raised both hands above her head and brought them down among the paraphernalia. Something shattered with a crash and sprayed small parts into the darkness.

Emilio tapped Dario on the shoulder to get his attention and then motioned for him to go to the left of the girl. He pulled out his knife—a commando blade he'd gotten from a guy who'd been in the army—and pointed to his own chest. The message was clear: Emilio himself would take down the woman.

They walked across the room as silently as they could, even though it looked like the woman was in a world of her own and wouldn't have heard them if they'd approached beating drums. Was she actually performing some kind of satanic rite? Did anyone really believe in that stuff, nearly two decades into the twenty-first century?

His heart beat faster and faster as he approached. He'd never killed anyone in cold blood before, and never imagined that his first would be a woman. But there were unwritten rules about what could and couldn't be delegated to underlings within the deeply hierarchal world of the *barras bravas*—Argentina's soccer hooligans.

About four feet away, he took a deep breath and charged forward. Without hesitation, he covered the woman's mouth with one hand to keep her from screaming and drew the razor-sharp blade across her throat in one violent motion with the other. The knife dug deep, briefly caught on something, then slid along. Blood spurted onto his wrist.

Only after the woman stopped struggling did Emilio stop to think. Something felt wrong. It took him a second to realize what it was: the woman's mouth. It was covered with something.

He looked down at the dead body and pulled his hand away. His victim had been soundly gagged with silver tape.

And he recognized her. It was a face that had been on every TV set in the country for nearly three days: a young high-schooler who'd

3

disappeared on her way home earlier in the week. Everyone suspected she'd been kidnapped.

An icy ball formed in his stomach as he studied her. The rags she was wearing had once been a grey school uniform. Her hands were tied together, which explained why she'd been waving them above her arms. Her bare feet were swollen and purple: he suspected that someone had broken the bones to keep her from attempting to stand.

She'd been placed there as bait for a trap he'd fallen right into.

"Dario, let's get out of here now," Emilio said.

Before his companion could respond, bright lights shone into his eyes, blinding him.

"Now!" Emilio yelled and ran for the only thing he could see: the door and the sunlight beyond it.

As he left the building, Emilio turned to look for Dario, but the other man wasn't there. Out in the open, his sudden fear disappeared, and the man who'd faced countless numbers of opposing fans in one brawl after another was back in control.

But the confidence was short-lived.

Behind him, a scream began. It started out as a man's yell, but gradually increased in pitch as the victim was subjected to unbearable pain. Then it turned ragged and finally, just… stopped. He strained his ears to hear more, but there was no more to come.

Dario.

Emilio ran. He took off down the filthy path, turned muddy by the human waste that flowed down its center. His feet struggled to gain purchase with every step, and he had to concentrate on keeping his balance. The dazed inhabitants of the shantytown turned their heads to watch him pass, but he ignored them.

Pursuit was never far behind. He could hear the footsteps of the men behind him, multiple pairs. He had no illusions regarding the possibility of being able to deal with them. He was very much the visiting team here, and the men he would be facing if he faltered were hard men, used to living a criminal life… just like he was.

His breath grew labored.

Where is the exit? The muddy paths seemed to twist into each other, the houses all looked the same—the inhabitants expended no energy in making them different—and offered no landmarks. Still, he knew that if he ran fast enough, and turned often enough, pursuit would falter; in fact, the footsteps behind him seemed to be getting further and further away.

He made another sharp turn and put on a burst of speed. It was a calculated risk: he expended his very last reserves to do it, but knew that his pursuers would never be able to guess which way he'd gone.

Then Emilio stopped suddenly.

Right in front of him was a familiar structure: a concrete tower with a gaping empty door. He knew the door led into a dark room with the body of a murdered girl inside.

"So good of you to come back to us," an old lady said.

This one did look like a witch. Scraggly grey hair framed rheumy eyes, and her smile held more gaps than teeth. She nodded and two men appeared beside Emilio.

He turned to face one, but the other must have hit him in the back of the head with something. Blackness beckoned.

"So, you boys are from the River Plate crowd?" The voice croaked and rattled.

Emilio opened an eye. The pain in his head was almost unbearable, but he struggled to come fully awake. The old woman was seated in front of him.

He tried to move, but his arms were firmly tied behind his back. Likewise, his ankles had been silver-taped to his chair. He could see the tape by craning his neck.

He spat and the spittle landed in a pile of half-congealed blood. The girl's body had been pushed to one side, a gruesome rag doll, but the blood was still pooled where it had fallen, and his chair seemed to be right in the middle of it. There was no sign of Dario.

He tried to talk, but the reply caught in his throat and he gagged. The coughing turned to retching and dry heaves. Nearly a minute passed before he was in control of his body again. The old lady watched him impassively, ugly eyes boring into him. He glared back.

"I suppose you must be. That's good. We can watch the match together. Would you like that?"

He spat at her.

Instead of anger, she merely smiled, stood and patted his arm.

"I'll be back in time for the game," she said, and disappeared behind him.

5

Emilio looked around the room. There was nothing in it, other than the body of the girl he'd killed and the pool of blood. As the afternoon wore on, the light from the doorway dimmed before finally disappearing completely, leaving him with only the dim yellow light from the bulb for company.

He thought about screaming for help, but remembered the vacant faces of the inhabitants of the slum. They wouldn't get involved, and the police probably hadn't been this deep in the shantytown since the lands were first overrun by the poor. He would gain nothing from yelling but the possibility of another beating. At the very least, if he stayed silent, he wouldn't lose his honor.

A noise behind him made him turn. Two men were wheeling a large TV screen mounted on a table into the room. A small boy behind them had a long extension cable looped around his arm.

The old woman walked over to him.

"You're lucky. You'll get to watch the game today."

He heard another cart rolling up behind him, but when he turned to see what it held, he couldn't spot it.

The men with the TV had finished setting it up. The image was grainy and of low quality, but good enough to see the players warming up on the field of play.

As the national anthem played and the players lined up in the middle of the field, the old woman sat cross-legged on the ground in front of him and, ignoring the dried blood, began to chant, slapping the concrete floor with her hands and swinging her head wildly from left to right. In the light of the bulb and the TV set, the effect was ethereal.

"I don't believe in any of this," he said loud enough for the men in the corners to hear him too. "You're just a fraud."

The old woman ignored him and continued for a few moments more. Then, with a final yell, she stopped and slowly picked herself up. She gave him a wide grin that allowed him an excellent view of the few rotting teeth that remained to her. "The good thing is that you don't need to believe for it to work."

The players were taking their places on the field. The woman walked around him three times then stopped behind him, where he couldn't see, but he heard the sound of metal against metal. They must have rolled some kind of cart loaded with things up to his back. He swallowed, remembering how easy it had been to slit the girl's throat, and wondered if he would soon share her fate. He swallowed and kept his eyes on the screen.

The match had started. If Dario had been in his place, the spectacle of watching River playing the hated Boca team would have been enough to make him forget his predicament; for a couple of hours, he would have forgotten all about the fact that he was tied to a chair. His life's one consuming passion was the River soccer team... and that truly superseded anything else. He fought against the fans of other teams for reasons that might best be described as religious. Not accepting that River was the pinnacle of existence was, to Dario, heresy.

Emilio differed. He was a casual soccer fan at best. His concerns had more to do with the power that could be achieved—even from humble beginnings—among the fan organizations. One worked one's violent way up the ladder, from the fringes and dope dealers all the way to the center, literally the center, of the main grandstand, which was where the bosses of the *barra* held sway, the men who received the payoffs to provide muscle to political campaigns and who controlled the drug dealing in vast swathes of the Buenos Aires metropolitan area. As the camera panned over the spectators, he wondered if anyone missed him, or whether some lower-ranked lieutenant was already using his absence to try to get that one step closer to the top.

The woman walked back into his line of sight. She was holding a long, thin knife.

"I'm not afraid of you," he said.

"I don't care about that. Those macho games are things men play among themselves. I'm sure my companions over there are very impressed, but I have other duties." She sliced into his shirt, removing a square of cloth above Emilio's stomach. She spoke while she worked. "I wasn't always a witch, you know. Once, I was a doctor. A thoracic surgeon, to be precise. But they sent me to jail for harvesting organs. They said that my patients would not have died except for my negligence. They said I'd killed them for personal profit."

The old woman spat and turned to watch the game. It was still scoreless, so she sat cross-legged and observed the match in silence.

Not having any other choice, Emilio watched with her.

About twenty minutes into the first half, River scored a goal. He screamed the word *goal* as loudly as he could. He might be the prisoner of the rival faction, but he wouldn't show them that he was afraid, despite the crawling sensation in his stomach.

He expected the big guys to beat him to a pulp, but instead, it was the woman who reacted. "This is too bad," she said, shaking her head sadly.

Getting back to her feet with difficulty, she approached him.

"I never killed a patient in my life, and negligence… I was the best surgeon in Argentina. No one died needlessly on my watch. They were all selling the organs of the dead patients, but they came after me because I was a woman."

She poked a finger into his stomach, and for some reason that single gesture brought all his fear to the fore. It was all he could do to control his bladder.

"I learned to control the spirits in jail. Have you ever been to jail? I don't think so. The *barras* have politicians behind them. You never go to jail, do you? In jail, you need power, and the way I got it was by befriending a witch. She taught me what she knew… and she took her price."

"I don't believe in any of that."

"I already told you. What you believe doesn't matter." Without any expression, she made an incision all the way across his stomach, just above the belly button, from left to right.

Emilio screamed. He screamed until his world was nothing but screams and then he screamed again. Finally, he gathered himself enough to ask: "What are you doing?"

"Nothing you believe in," the witch replied. She gestured to one of the men behind him. Tough hands took him by the hair and wrapped tape around his head several times, covering his mouth comprehensively. "Now you need to be quiet. You wouldn't want me to lose my concentration and kill you by mistake, now would you?"

She started playing with the loose folds of skin and Emilio looked away. Unable to scream, the pain seemed somehow worse. He writhed in the chair. Blood soaked his pants.

When he looked down, the old woman was holding something in her hands that looked like a snake. With horror, he realized that it came from within him: a length of his entrails. This time, he couldn't control his bladder—or anything else.

He must have passed out because her voice in his ear brought him back to consciousness. "The first incantation worked wonderfully," she said. "Opening you up for the spirits has made them receptive to my spell. I asked them to give me something in return, and they did. Look."

The score was one to one.

The woman patted him on the shoulder. "But you don't believe in any of that, of course." She sat by the TV, watching intently. "Let's see how it goes from here."

He felt weak, but somehow managed to stay awake for the halftime interval and the beginning of the second half.

The woman spoke again. "For most spells, animal offal, mainly from chickens, is enough. The spirits aren't greedy. Small attentions suffice." The she turned to the screen showing the most important soccer match in the country, one of the most important anywhere in the world. A game that millionaires from Europe flew in to see, and that was consistently ranked among the top can't-miss sporting events by the world press: Boca-River, the Superclasico. "But some things are too big for that. They demand more."

She watched the game in silence for some minutes. Time was running out, with only ten minutes remaining in the second half.

"Well, I guess it's now or never." The woman returned to him and, pausing only to reach over his shoulder to pick up a plastic bottle of alcohol, began to pull at his entrails, slopping them into a pile at his feet. He screamed into the gag, but there was nothing he could do. Blood spurted in every direction. How was it possible for him to remain conscious? Shouldn't he have lost too much blood?

He felt his consciousness slipping but fought to stay awake.

The witch-woman doused the pile of guts, still connected to his body, with alcohol. He couldn't understand why she was trying to keep him disinfected. Would that save his life? Surely, she couldn't put all of that back in, could she? Whatever the answer was, she emptied the entire bottle onto his entrails.

Then she looked up and, apparently surprised to see that he was conscious, gave him a rotting smile. "It would probably be better for you not to watch this next part." In a single fluid motion, she struck a match and dropped it.

Foomp!

The alcohol caught fire and the smell of cooking meat reached him.

Emilio screamed and screamed. He couldn't feel the pain from his stomach, but his legs were on fire.

A noise from the TV caused him to look up. Yellow-and-blue-clad players were hugging each other in celebration. Boca had scored a goal.

The score was two to one when the referee blew the final whistle. River, the club he loved and to whose hard-core fans Emilio belonged, had lost.

After that, everything went dark.

The Fourth

M. M. De Voe

WHEN LORD ZHYKLON INVITED ME to the head table to play an ancient game with him, I felt blessed. I thought it proved my worth. My father had tutored me intensely in chess and Go and several other old strategy games, and so far in my twenty-six years, this ability had never been of any use except to attract gamer boyfriends. And girlfriends. I'm not that picky when it comes to the bits—I'm more attracted to what's between the ears. Frankly, I was so sick of being seen as a trophy (cute girl who's smart? I win!) that when the summons came—in the form of an enchanted scroll on human skin, of course— I accepted immediately, even though it radiated pure evil. Yes, I knew that no one ever survived a meeting with Lord Zhyklon. Sure, I was vastly uncomfortable with touching the scroll at all, human rights and fair trade and all that stuff you pick up at a liberal arts college, but I figured if I could handle myself with rival lovers on the same panel at a werewolf con in Idaho, I could damned well face whatever foul creature had asked me to burn a black candle and chant its name three times while inverting my eyelids and licking my lips.

No easy task, mind you. I wasn't allowed to use my hands to invert my eyelids. Took a while to get it. But I can also tie a cherry stem with my tongue without cheating, so there's that.

Anyway.

One of my exes—a balding, twice-divorced guy with a neon green Vespa—was avidly into Pathfinder, GURPS, and D&D, so I knew my

11

way around role-play. This likely also explains why I hadn't immediately taken my own life once I realized the spell had worked and I was trapped in an evil alternate reality. I initially regained consciousness in an opulent 18th-century locked bedchamber, holding only my dead cellphone instead of the creepy scroll I'd been chanting from while LiveTweeting the ceremony.

I did not hesitate to toss the now-useless phone onto the brocade bedspread and immediately change into the old-fashioned corset I found set out for me there. I tightened the laces, pulled on the multiple petticoats, the hoop frame, more petticoats, then the yellow satin dress. Believe me, I'd done my share of roleplay for both genders—I knew what was expected. Scrambling over to the mirror, I did my hair in an updo from the 1800s I'd learned for cosplay and placed the curls fetchingly across my forehead. Then I checked once again if there was phone signal (the phone wouldn't even turn on) and also to see if the windows were locked (they were), and set about assessing my situation.

I discovered that I was in a tower on an extremely high floor, and furthermore that, although one of the two windows budged open a sliver, the glass panes were tragically unbreakable. I tried the door and received not only another dose of pure evil, but also a relatively severe electric shock. This caused me to return to the window-seat. Believe me, I needed to sit down.

Was the geography that spread off into the distance within my normal universe but at a different time and place, or was I in another dimension altogether? I had already made value judgments based on the décor: the two tapestries showed a white male knight in glowing armor being snapped in half by giant crab claws, and a screaming girl torn in thirds by competing octopi. *Patriarchal Old Europe*, I thought, and therefore I sat with ankles demurely crossed, the provided yellow slippers on my feet. In the distance there were thick evergreens, half-subsuming snow-capped mountains. No other dwellings were visible, though birds of prey sometimes circled through the clouds. The occasional raven laughed as it wheeled past my tower.

Despite the seemingly Alpine surroundings, this castle or multi-turreted mansion (it was hard to tell from my beautiful prison) appeared to live in the middle of a swamp. I say live because who knows? We've all heard stories of sentient castles eating their inhabitants and so forth, and clearly I wasn't in some remote place in my usual dimension. Not only did my cellphone not work, but gravity seemed slightly lessened since I could easily glide across the floor as befitted a maiden in some 18th century alternate reality. Not that I was actually a maiden by patriarchal European definition, but okay; I was young enough and I was cisgender female. By craning my neck, I could just glimpse brackish water and various shadowy reptilian shapes gliding by. Through the small opening in the window, I could also smell an ocean nearby, though my deep calming breaths were often interrupted by startling wisps of methane and sulfur. Occasionally, too, I heard the nearby barking of frenzied hounds as if just before a feeding, but otherwise the atmosphere was quiet, with just the ravens' mocking cries to break the silence.

Time passed. I was fed after a long interval—the food was plentiful and simple, served in the style of an ancient English hunting manor, meaning that my reluctantly shed tears held more salt than either the gravy or the meat. The tray had been brought in by a serving boy, and I thought I might find an ally in him. He appeared human. His eyes were brown and intelligent. He was too young to have been here long. His blond mustache was wispy as if he had not yet been taught to shave. His hair was in a low ponytail and reached the center of his back. He wore clothing reminiscent of someone's 18th century fantasy of the Orient—gold genie pants and slippers that curled up at the toes, with a purple sash and white, blousy sleeves. The outfit looked a bit stupid and I thought I might be able to win his confidence by joking with him about the garb and décor. But I soon discovered that he was not interested in friendship.

He hovered over me until I had returned every piece of china and cutlery to its proper place on the tray. Having nothing to lose, I tried frankness.

"Think I could hold onto this knife, for defense?" I asked.

He wasn't willing to collude.

And he had sharp observation skills. After I finished the watery custard provided for dessert, my wrist was held in a superhuman grip as he twisted the demitasse spoon free and replaced it gently on the tray.

I begged the servant boy not to tell his master what I had done, promised I would help him escape in return, but he only gave me a half-hearted grin in reply. And there I saw my error.

An oily, dark, greenish liquid seeped through his bared teeth, and I moved swiftly back to my window seat in an attempt to hide my disgust and, frankly, fear. He wasn't human. Or at least he wasn't human like I was. I was left alone for twelve hours, wherein I discovered there were no secret panels in the walls, no trapdoors under the elaborate rugs, and not one of the books in the large bookcase opened to a secret escape route. Additionally, the books were all in languages I couldn't read. I was initially happy just to see that books existed in this world, but I soon discovered that it was torture to run my fingers over shelves of accessible knowledge that I couldn't extract.

Not one of the books had pictures.

So, back to the window with me.

There was only one moon, bright enough to erase any constellations that could have helped me know where I was located. Without that app on my phone as reference, however, astrology wouldn't have helped. I doubted this world had the Big Dipper or Orion. Even if it did, what would that tell me? I could no sooner find a physical way out of this castle than teleport.

When being held captive in a patriarchal alternate universe, it's never a good idea to show fear. Even when your wrists and ankles are shackled and you're being led down a long stone staircase to a rank dungeon where the clammy air has not moved for centuries. Even when you see that your cellmate is roped to the wall, his torso torn open, innards dripping down to his feet. You do not complain of the stench. You do not quake. You press your tongue to the roof of your mouth the way you learned in acting class, to activate your eyes while breathing through your nose, leaving your lips relaxed. You don't show your true emotions. Even when you're left there, in the darkness, in your ridiculous yellow gown, without a word. You maintain the role. It seems like you have no other choice—though you recognize that you always have a choice. Acting this way prolongs your life and you very much value your life.

You do wonder, however, at your own gullible nature. I had responded to a request to play a game with someone calling himself Lord Zhyklon. It had never occurred to me that this most basic premise might be a lie. I hadn't considered that the invitation itself might be a trick. I'd only recognized that the person doing the inviting was obviously evil. I'd considered the possibility of abduction, torture, and imprisonment, once the game had been played, but not of the simple lie that there might not even be a game.

Thus, when, many months later, a beast filled the doorway of my subterranean cell—a beast I could smell before seeing, a beast that undulated and swarmed, that blinded me with a fear so great I was sure my head was splitting open—to welcome me to his castle and invite me to be the fourth at a game he was playing upstairs, I was relieved rather than horrified. It made me feel briefly delighted that it hadn't been a trick after all.

I get that this is stupid, but still and all.

I was briefly delighted.

I was.

I fell immediately back into the role-playing nature I had abandoned after months in this dank cell, and knew instinctively that the proper thing to do when confronted by a patriarchal creature from a literal Hell, was not to scream in terror, but to curtsey as low as possible, forehead touching the filthy flagstones, and kindly accept with an *as you please, m'lord,* keeping my eyes lowered. Because first-off, anyone whose father was a Lovecraftian literary scholar in a third-rate community college knows never to look into any god's eyes, and secondly, no one is ever polite anymore, and a polite young person might just get ahead in the world. You never know.

Also, it is easier to breathe near the floor.

Anyway, and I'm ashamed to admit this, it was kind of... well... flattering. It was obvious that few mortals were ever allowed to play with him and even fewer humans. And when you add that I'm a female specimen and this was a Chthulu-esque world, well, it suddenly seemed to me, let's say, a kind of weird honor that he chose me of all the meat puppets in the multiverse. He turned, clearly expecting me to follow, moving fast for someone with no legs. I hiked up my filthy skirts as best I could and ran after him. The steps were slippery, but the thick slime trail he left made it easy to see where to go. My worn yellow slippers were greenish by the time I reached the top. Forty-seven steps up from the dungeons, twenty-six across the flagstone landing, another thirty to the subterranean ballroom where he held game night.

My wet feet were cold—the stone floors seemed to radiate right through the lousy slippers—but I'm certain the pallor this gave my skin would be pleasing to the dank lord. I thought maybe Hastur the Unspeakable or one of the other Great Old Ones would be playing, but no, the room held only a couple of Swedish minions. Could be that the original fourth had been eaten, or killed, or died of fright, or possibly madness took him. But I'm going with Hastur blowing off the invitation. No one seems to honor RSVPs anymore, even in interdimensional pocket universes, even for something as intimate as game night. And according to my dad's endless ramblings, Chthulu's half-brother Hastur is notorious for being irritating for no reason. It seems to me that not showing up to a four-person gaming session is just his kind of thing. Funny, I used to roll my eyes when dad would start on some Lovecraftian gabbling in the car or at dinner, and out of love or dismay, he often stopped the lecture.

How I wished now that I had listened!

I missed my dad with a squeezing, empty pain. He probably would have enjoyed this whole thing despite the "you are going to inevitably die or go mad" ending. He used to say that a person can set his mind to enjoy just about anything.

I decided to try.

Climbing up to the dais where the three beings sat at an enormous wooden table with spiral legs, I avoided the pools of seawater and greenish-gray slime as best I could. The stench was unspeakable, but no worse than I was used to in the dungeons. The familiar servant boy unshackled my wrists, which allowed me to properly curtsey to the minions. I took some pleasure in knowing that I was role-playing exactly as they expected.

I looked forward to beating them at whatever game they were playing.

The two Swedes bobbed their oversized heads. The six eyes on either side of their carpish heads rolled independently of each other. Their lips gaped and closed to the ceiling, and the female seemed to be trying to blow spit bubbles that kept popping. I wasn't sure if this was a sign of respect or disgust, so I repeated my curtsey to each of the Deep Ones in turn, not wanting to offend. The female of the pair ruffled her back spikes. The male waved a twelve-pointed fin. I drew a relieved breath. The air tasted like cold herring.

I've never liked cold herring. Never liked seafood of any kind, truth be told.

"I'm eager to start the game, m'Lord," I said.

The fishy people stared at me.

Lord Zhyklon finally waved a tentacle as if to beckon me to the table, and I took my place in the last of the tall, straight-backed velvet chairs. Zhyklon did not stand for a lady. It made my head ache to think about how his smooth, dripping skin stood at all, or how the impossible shape I had seen in the dungeon had contorted itself into a human chair. Throne, really, with swirling ebony pinnacles that blended with the garden of foggy tentacles sprouting from the ancient one's head. I lowered my eyes to the game board and placed my hands flat upon the table as seemed proper.

Keep your hands where we can see 'em, and all that.

European Rampage was a game I had never played, and I hoped the rules wouldn't be too complicated. The board was simply a detailed map of Europe crafted of wrought iron with gold filigree. There were no borders indicated, although London, Frankfurt, Vienna, Minsk, St. Petersburg, and other familiar cities were marked with large rubies. The smaller cities—Copenhagen, Oslo, Zagreb, Dublin—were marked with emeralds. There were scattered sapphires as well, and I wished I had a working smartphone so that I could identify them.

The servant boy, having shackled my ankles to my chair, stood in a contorted position on a cushion made of the pale tanned skins of some unknown creature. I was reminded of the Venus de Milo, though this boy's hands were intact. In them, he held a thick scroll, which he unwound as he read the rules to the game. His voice was a soporific monotone, a torture I had not anticipated, and one that grated more than the shackles, which had a vague S/M titillating aspect.

On and on he droned while green ooze trickled over his chin and down his neck.

While he was reading these endless rules, a snake-man appeared tableside, counted out gold and silver coins, and placed the stacks at my right hand. I'm embarrassed to admit this, but I grew excited. It looked like real money. I touched it. It was. I don't know how a person can tell when foreign money is real, but perhaps it's an innate human trait. I knew without doubt that this money was real. Fifty gold and thirty silver coins: a fortune to a girl who had grown up the daughter of a non-tenured academic. What was I thinking? That I would win the game and go home wealthy? I will tell you that at this point, I suddenly stopped being afraid and looked for the positive side of my predicament. Yes, I was about to join a horribly boring-sounding game with three creatures that seemingly did not speak. But friends: the corn chips in the crystal bowls had not been bought on sale at a Costco.

17

They were probably organic. From non-GMO corn. Artisanal corn chips, individually hand-crafted and fried in some exotic healthful oil.

If there was such a thing.

And this snack had been laid out on this crazy table for whom?

For me, that's whom.

I was the whom.

Not the girlfriend. The gamer.

Me.

And I was damned near unbeatable at board games.

A deep rumbling, like an ocean vortex engulfing a ship with all its doomed sailors screaming, emitted from the ancient being at the head of the table. The sound snapped my attention back to the accounting of the various intricacies of game strategies possible within the complicated rule set, even as a blinding light behind my eyes caused me to wince in pain. I had forgotten that Lord Zhyklon was likely to be able to read minds.

More than an hour I sat, spine erect, fighting the competing stenches of rotting moss and corn chips, palms pressing hard on the table in the hopes that it would keep my eyelids open, as the servant droned the rules. The game was extremely complicated: one had to purchase lengths of pipe to allow liquid to travel from metropolis to metropolis, and the labor to build these pipes cost more when crossing rivers, mountains, or boundaries of populated locations. There were various event cards including avalanches, floods, intentional explosions, dissatisfied work forces, mass starvations, opioid drug use, hailstorms, taxes…. I already hated this game with a passion. Why could the king of madness not have chosen something light and fast like Sushi Go or Exploding Kittens?

I could only hope to play better than his minions without actually beating him. I needed to earn his respect and perhaps he would release me, though hopefully not impregnated or insane. When the reading of the rules finally ended, I briefly released my palms and found them whiter than a vampire's victim from the pressure I had needed to exert to stay awake.

The game began.

Lord Zhyklon, of course, went first. He thought for a long time, debating where to lay his first pipes. Waving tentacles obscured the ceiling, shuffling and twitching as he sorted through various possibilities. The Swedes went next, each also debating several moves before placing their first length of pipe. I was sure that more than an hour had passed before my turn.

This was a torture worse than flaying. If every turn went this way, I would age faster than the game could end.

Six hours later, I was certain of my doom. I had laid a pipe to Gdansk and discovered that I didn't have enough silver to even bribe another player on the cheap, which was in itself an unreliable strategy. In gameplay, I was stuck, incapable of earning, incapable of winning. There was no way out. No safety clause. No release. I was in eternal torment, which the other three players either failed to notice or failed to find important. It then occurred to me that as their fourth, I had made it possible for them to end their game, otherwise it would continue indefinitely. They were immortals. I was not. At some point I would die and in doing so, I would forfeit and their game would come to a satisfying conclusion. They would tally up the money they had earned and declare a winner. All was contingent on me, my constitution. As the only mortal player, I was brought food at intervals, and was allowed the usual breaks for evacuations and to go to the samovar to refill my glass. The tea had properties that kept me alert; by now, days had gone by without sleep.

I could not win, I could not lose. I could not complain. I could only exist another day. And then another.

This was actually living hell.

The worst was the silence. The Swedes jostled each other when their turns ended. Lord Zhyklon himself allowed the servant boy to play his pieces so that he would not slime the board. But I? I was required to play my own turn.

All the chance had left this game long ago. Zhyklon and his minions were amassing wealth at a snail's pace. My presence was irrelevant. I was only the fourth at the table, the timer, the dummy. I moved along the pipes, back and forth, back and forth, between Gdansk and Lisbon, sometimes stopping in Milan. Back and forth, back and forth. I regretted breaking up with each of my exes, particularly the clever computer guy who wasn't particularly good looking but oh how funny he was. I longed for the endless hours of D&D where my elven mage's unconscious body was hidden away safely, awaiting a resurrection spell while I ate Cheetos and watched my forty-year-old boyfriend's ranger fight the Drow. At least in that game, there had been a goal. At least there, the players talked.

The corset bit into my waist and hips. My feet had blistered inside my wet slippers, which would clearly never dry in this dank room. I kept my swollen, aching mind on the game, though tears welled up whenever my turn came. My hands had picked up a tremor and shook as I moved the piece its limited nine lengths. Releasing the token, I gasped for air, certain that I was starting to look more and more like one of the immortal Deep Ones. This game would never end. I could quit and be killed, I supposed, but the one time I allowed myself to think it, one of Zhyklon's many eyes darted my way and narrowed—and I knew that I wanted to live as long as possible.

I could only play. It was my turn again, and again I moved nine paces toward a city that I could not affect. I swayed in my chair, my mind unraveling. I could not win, I could not lose, I could only play. Madness, then. My father had said that stories set in this world always ended in madness or death.

But I wanted agency. If I was going to die or go mad, it would be by my own hand, not some unspeakable god's bizarre will.

It was Zhyklon's turn again. I turned to the Swede closer to me and blew her a kiss.

"Hey. When this game is over, you want to play double solitaire up in my room?"

The other Swede gasped for air and his body slid off the chair. One of his tiny finlike hands clutched at the edge of the game board, and caught. The map tipped towards the Deep One and all the many, many carefully laid pipes and piles of gold and silver avalanched to the floor, splashing in the seawater puddles, rolling across the ornate rug, sticking to the slime. Lord Zhyklon towered over the offender, his skin rippling into a ghastly red that reminded me of the blood on the pelt of a flayed rabbit. His anger was a palpable yellow gas that emerged from pores in his skin. It smelled of dead things and I could see the eyes of the Swede on the floor widen as death took him.

Unfortunately, the emissions continued, unabated, as Lord Zhyklon shrieked and tore the Swede into strips of white flesh and let them fall to the floor. The female Swede died second, gasping like a goldfish. Lord Zhyklon, intent on disemboweling her mate, ignored her.

Evil swept the room.

As the darkness closed in around me, I slipped into a satisfied unconscious swoon. No one ever survived a meeting with Lord Zhyklon, I had known that when I accepted the challenge. I would be killed along with the Deep Ones—there was no question, had never been any question—but I would die smiling. And I wouldn't have to play another minute of that horribly boring and pointless game. And that meant that, in a way, I had won.

Killer Shot
Ann Stolinsky

BARS HAVE A REPUTATION for being noisy. McRyan's fits that stereotype.

Big, burly men sat at one end of the bar, chugging their beers. Boys who wanted to be men sat at the other end, their butts barely covering the bar stools, nursing their lite beers. And, interspersed in each group, the women.

Some beauties sat with each group, laughing and batting their eyelashes. Boys and men alike grabbed their wallets and bought them drinks, hoping to take one of the women home with them.

And then there are the women who were not spectacular beauties, buying their own drinks.

I won't say which group was the happiest, nor into which I fit.

Dim lighting couldn't permeate the smoke-filled interior, wisps snaking their way into each patron's lungs. The pool table stood prominently under a fluorescent light fixture. The sound of the off-key live band masked the click of a cue stick hitting the billiard balls.

My eyes were drawn, as they always were, to the dart board hanging on the south wall. Pinholes in the panels surrounding the target highlighted patrons' blissful misjudgments. I smiled. I had been one of those patrons who missed the mark but a few months ago. No longer.

I ignored the distractions surrounding me, dart in my right hand, its tail between my thumb and forefinger. Not too tight, not too loose. Just right, like Baby Bear's porridge in the Goldilocks story.

My hand dropped to my side as a fool wandered directly into my line of sight. His ambling didn't disturb me. Once he was past, I focused again on the dart board, on the black circle in the middle, bringing my hand back and forth slightly, almost imperceptibly, tuning out the ambiance once more.

The bullseye almost didn't exist—others' lucky shots had occasionally punctured it. I chipped away at the rest of the bullseye. The experience of practicing taught me a lot in the last few months— how to wait patiently for the right moment to attack, how to focus on my target as if it, and only it, existed in the room.

I aimed and let the dart soar. Another bullseye.

"Are you ready?"

I inhaled deeply, smoothed down my skirt, and exhaled.

"Yes, I am."

I stepped back as my lawyer opened the double doors toward me. After he affixed them on each side, he joined me. We walked in together, my head high, eyes focused on the empty bench before me. We strode to the victim's table and sat. The courtroom was filled with the best and worst of humanity. Worst of all was the defendant.

The bailiff entered from a door in the front of the room.

"All rise."

My eyes followed the man in the robes as he ambled from his chambers to the bench. He sat; so did we.

"Miss Stone, are you ready?"

My lawyer turned to me, his hand steady on my chair as I pushed it back. His eyes met mine. He stood when I did. We turned to the judge simultaneously.

"I am, Your Honor."

"The jury has declared the defendant guilty on all counts. The court has heard your victim's statement and agrees with your lawyer that you have the right to decide the defendant's fate."

I nodded.

"While the sentence rendered by the jury is death, the law provides for alternate methods of delivering the sentence when the conviction is for violent crimes against minors. While you are no longer a minor, the despicable actions by the defendant were perpetrated upon you when you were. The law clearly states that when a victim has reached maturity, that victim is allowed to determine the fate of the convicted.

If you were still a minor, your mother would be tasked with this choice. In this case, Miss Stone, the court will abide by your decision. You will determine whether the criminal is to die by your hand, giving the convicted a possibility of life in prison instead, or if death is to come quickly by the actions of the court."

I smiled. I knew which choice was preferable.

"Death, Your Honor. By my hand."

"You do realize your choice affords him the chance to survive, to live out his last days in prison."

"Yes, Your Honor. I know."

He was handcuffed, his legs chained together. He fidgeted on the seat, set in the middle of a vinyl pool. Six-foot round, sides three-foot high. A pool out of place in this setting, a pool that should have been found in a backyard with children splashing in it, or at a carnival with a bell attached rather than a black mylar balloon.

The pool stood in a room separated from the audience by glass. Everyone present would be able to see the events as they happened.

The judge called my name. My lawyer walked with me over to the bailiff.

"Are you sure this is what you want to do? If you miss, he gets life in prison instead of the justice he deserves."

"I'm sure. And I won't miss."

The bailiff ushered me through the door to another room, enclosed by glass, except for one, four-foot-wide and six-foot-high empty space where a pane had been removed. *This is sufficient for me.*

The bailiff handed me a dart. One solitary dart. One instrument of death, or renewal of life if I missed. I held it for a few seconds, getting the feel of it, assessing the weight. I looked the bastard straight in the eyes—fear showed in his, but I knew there was strength in mine.

"You can't do it," he sneered. "You know you can't."

My training at the bar paid off. I ignored the distractions, the whispers from the gallery, his alternating pleas and taunts.

"You liked it," his voice rose as his face reddened. "You were a willing participant. You walked around the house with your skimpy shorts and your boobs hanging out of your tank tops. You brought teenage boyfriends home and I saw how they touched your ass." He tried sitting forward, struggled to be released from his bonds.

My calm infuriated and humiliated him.

25

"You asked for it, you whore!"

He began to shake, his anger and fear producing a physical reaction.

"You can't do this—you *love* me. I was more of a father than the bastard who spawned you!

"FUCK YOU!" he screamed.

I drew my hand back and forth several times as he ranted, aiming the dart. It left my hand as he spoke his last word, its tip elegant in flight. Silence. Then one explosive sound—the pop of the balloon as the dart found its target. His sneer turned to shock, his mouth agape. A lever on the seat, held up only by the balloon, was released. Liquid rained down from the balloon, water bubbling as the two compounds mixed together. The seat tilted forward. Sliding down, his shackled feet bicycled furiously, trying to gain purchase. In seconds, his feet stopped moving as the acid touched his clothing and his skin. It took several seconds for him to be totally submerged, and a few minutes for the acid to finish the job.

The bailiff opened the door to the little room, encouraging me to depart. I looked back at the pool and smiled.

"No, you're fucked."

I walked to the exit without a backward glance.

McRyan's was crowded that night. I was elated that my trauma was over, and I could begin to heal. I wouldn't have to look over my shoulder all the time, wondering, worrying, if he was behind me. I smiled. I could begin to live.

The dart hit the bullseye once again.

A guy I didn't recognize walked toward me.

"Betcha five bucks you can't get another bullseye."

I glanced at him, then let the dart fly.

"Hey, good shot!"

"Thanks." I smiled as I reached for his money. "It's my killer shot."

Hide and Seek

Daniel Arthur Smith

WHEN YOU CHOOSE TO LIVE your life interstellar, run-ins with an acquaintance from one's formative years become rare to nonexistent. Hansen is such an old friend, which is to say that we've known each other since we were small children, attended public preparatory together, and even shared the first years of junior college. So when a hand delivered message arrived to inform me that he was planet-side, I didn't hesitate to accept the invitation to visit him in his penthouse suite.

His penthouse, I should mention, was at the top of the Lassiter Grand, a five-star luxury hotel, which is itself within the pinnacle fifty floors of Providence Six's newest chromium luxury tower, The Chamreal. I'd be lying if I refused to admit that the location alone made the invitation all the more enticing. Please don't think me shallow; it wasn't the luxury suite that drew my keen interest, rather *how* it was that Hansen came to be a resident. You see, he was from a fine family, no questioning that, but not one of vast means, so I knew that whatever circumstances had brought him to his new station would be intriguing to say the least. So it was that the following night found me in the turbo-lift of the Lassiter Grand with a bottle of the best Providence Six had to offer in hand, ascending to her upmost floor.

Already, I was dazzled with the style and taste of the hotel, from the mammoth palm fronds throughout the atrium lobby to the darkened wood trim and intricately detailed red velvet paneling of the lift—all an homage to a simpler, colonial time. Even the rapid ascension of the transit was an elegant experience, lacking any sensation of motion; it was as if the cabin I'd stepped into remained in place while the world outside completely transformed. One moment, I was gazing upon that vast reflective marble floor of the jungle lobby; and the next, the scarlet carpet of the penthouse's cherry paneled anteroom—and the kind face of a beautiful young woman.

By the cerulean iridescence of her eyes, I assumed she was synthetic. Not that the neural lace that generates such a glow is exclusive to syns—out here it's quite common among mortals. I bear the blue glint myself. But from her manner and because she had donned the exquisitely tailored black coat and trousers of a butler, I presumed she was staff.

She greeted me with a bow of her head.

"Good evening, Mister Monroe," she said. "The master is waiting in the library."

"Excellent," I said, offering her the bottle. She took it in hand then, without waiting for me to say a word further, did an about face and proceeded to lead the way down the adjacent corridor. This hall was a wood paneled gallery in the same style as the lift and anteroom but decorated with oils of Earthen floral landscapes, their small ornately gilded frames accentuated by candle-bright amber sconces intermittently spaced between them. It was an interior meant to impress, and succeeded in doing so, but it was when I entered the master parlor that my jaw near fell agape, and not due to the books shelved floor to high ceiling along the side wall or the wide hearth of the working gas fireplace. No—though they too were indeed impressive. I was taken by the transparent outer wall, and beyond, the spectacular fuchsia nebula painting the Providence Six skyline.

Slowly, I moved forward, in awe of the gaseous wonder, and though I'd seen the ghost cloud of the nebula on few occasions before, nowhere near the surface was it presented as beautifully as it was framed here in this room.

"It's no mystery they call it *Eye of God*," said a matter of fact voice from the side of the room.

With a mix of surprise and embarrassment, I spun to see the owner of the proclamation. "Hansen," I said with as due exuberance as I could muster, "as I live and breathe."

"And you, Conrad, look at you," he said, approaching with arms extended. "You haven't changed a day."

Because we had both received our age mods some eighty years back at the fashionable age of twenty-two, it would have been quaint for me to mention that he hadn't changed either; it's rather stating the obvious, and he'd already spent the pleasantry. But embrace we did, as those set apart in this life tend to do on reunion, then rather than spend my compliment on him, I commented on the vista beyond. "I must tell you," I said, "the view from your parlor is exquisite."

"It's quite a location you've found yourself," he said, leading me closer to the transparent wall. "You have the contrast from the ancient," he dropped his gaze from the nebula to the neon laced darkness of the deep canyoned cityscape below, "to the modern."

Indeed, it was a contrast. The structures of the colony surrounding the super luxury towers were a hundred stories above the surface and burrowed yet another hundred or so more below, deep into the subterranean foundation of the original settlement, never touched by more than the light of a neon sky.

And there, gently floating thirty or so meters beneath, as if to punctuate our perch among the highest of the high, was a huge dirigible advertisement, her side brightly lit with an animated holo of the company's consoling geisha fairy—which reminded me. "Oh. Before I forget," I said. "I've brought some of the local elixir for you to enjoy during your visit."

His valet, still standing sentry at the door, stepped forward to present the label.

"*Providence Six, Elixir of Absinthe*," he read aloud. "To see through the *Eye of God*."

"Yes," I said. "So it proclaims. At any rate, highly enjoyable."

"I've heard that the recipe delivers an authentic sensation."

"You've heard correct. The recipe utilizes a synthetic form of wormwood, the key being that the thujone levels succeed in maintaining the *authentic* quality of the experience without the toxicity."

"And you prepare it in the fashion?"

"Exclusively."

"Brilliant. This aperitif will pair excellently with the planned entertainment. Alena, can you please make the preparations?"

Alena bowed her head and exited the parlor, leaving Hansen and I to resume our observation of the nebula beyond.

"Entertainment?" I asked. "What do you have in mind?"

"Something light. An accouterment of the hotel."

"Oh?"

"In a moment," he said. "First, you must tell me about the colonial life. What's it like out here on the perimeter?"

"I'm sorry to report that it's not far different than life back in the Homeland. I'm realizing at this moment I'm spending way too much time Mid-Hi, and not enough in the Upper."

"I'm sure," he said. "But the day to day is all consuming for the lot of us. Is it not?"

"Cheers. Yes. Well. As you sent your messenger, you must know that I'm a company man. My offices are fine, better than some. We do a fair amount of work with the Bureau, maintain the contracts with the mining consortium, the primary industry out here." I shrugged. "But, for the most part, it's mundane. Wine, women, and song, and all that."

"Cheers to wine, women, and song."

"Ha. Indeed. Life has been good but, as I age, there's a challenge to find vigor. I can't say I've embraced mediocrity, but then again, mediocrity has become redefined."

"How so?" he asked.

"I strive for, no, I have a thirst for excellence, even in my day to day."

"So, choosing not to settle. That's the key?"

"No small thing," I said. "If one wants to maintain the façade of enjoyment of life." It was when the words left my mouth that I realized the uncharacteristic candor with which I spoke. "Listen to me," I said apologetically. "Going dark when I should be elated to see an old friend such as yourself."

"But what are old friends without the spice of truth?" he kindly asked. "New topic. I see that we both have the cerulean tint in our eyes," he said, "from the neural lace."

"Yes," I answered. "I had mine implanted a few years back for a business trip far off-world."

"And just how far did you beam?"

"Farther than this mortal shell could easily travel. It's such a routine now. Popping out of one's shell and into another far and away. So much time saved. But you know this. You have your own."

"I do. Yes. Mine was implanted more recently, for the same reason—a trip to the Askar system."

"To the Askar. How fascinating," I said. "Which leads me to ask, how are *you* spending your time these days?"

For a brief moment I noticed that, though the features of his face had remained unchanged, there was a nuance, a confidence if you will, that had been absent in our youth.

"What you mean to ask," he said, "is how is it that I attained the status to warrant a stay in the master suite of the Lassiter Grand?"

"Excuse me for sounding so crass," I said, embarrassed he'd taken my query in such a way. "I didn't mean anything of the sort. I merely meant the same as your inquiry. You know? It's been decades since we've last—"

"It's all right," he said. The side of his mouth curled to a sly grin. "I'm having a laugh. Though, that is the question I want you to ask. It may be boorish, but unabashedly, the one I'd be asking. After all, of all of our year, I wouldn't have called me out as one to elevate beyond my station, to become an Arcadian."

"Now you're being harsh," I said, but the feat was indeed a curiosity, and one I myself had yet to achieve.

"No really," he said. "Martin maybe, Joston, who did in fact became an Arcadian. But me? Miles Hansen? Truth is, I have Melker to thank."

"Melker?" I said incredulously. "Benny Melker? I thought he hated you. I thought he hated everybody. He was always so…dreadful."

"Indeed. But it was his bullying, his constant reminder that I was lowborn—"

"Oh, come now."

"I know, I know. Of course, I was not—if anything, we were peers and in retrospect his family's holdings were scarcely different than my own. But all the same, it was his constant chastisement that drove me to succeed."

"I do apologize," I said. "It was all so long ago. Of course, I remember how inappropriately Benny behaved, but I never realized it would affect any one of us in any peculiar way. I always found him to be rather a gnat."

"A gnat?"

"Yes. A gnat. He'd come buzzing around, and we'd run the other way."

"Ironic. That's precisely my memory," he said. "Remember, and I'm going way back, but remember that game of Hide and Seek we used to play in the yards."

"Oh my. That is way back. We were, what, in our second, third year?"

"I suppose, but what I remember is Melker, running, red-faced. He hated that game."

"Yes," I said. "Fair enough. As I remember, he was inevitably *It*. We'd hide, he'd fight the devil finding us, and then could never keep up in the chase. No wonder he was such a tyrant. I wonder what ever happened to him."

"I dare say that I no longer care."

Hansen may have said he didn't care, but his stiff tone was contrary to the words and left me awkwardly stifled. Fortunately, it was at that moment Alena entered the parlor, wheeling the bar cart. She pushed it over near the fire, between two high backed, brown leather chairs. With a nod, Hansen gestured that we to should move to the fire. "Please," he said. "Have a seat." I circled the cart to sit in the interior chair then he relaxed into the other. As with the wood paneling, I couldn't tell if the leather was natural or synthetic, but it certainly had the scent and soft feel of the former.

Hansen sank back into his chair, but didn't appear to be at all comfortable. "Not quite right," he said.

"And what's that?" I asked.

"The fire," he said, then added, "Landon? Could you turn up the fire a smidge?"

With that, the flames increased in measure.

I inquired. "Landon is the—"

"The house butler," said Hansen. "It's better now. A bit cozier."

I'd never thought of my apartment's digital assistant as anything more than just that. A house AI with the ability to set your schedule or adjust the lights, temperature, and appliances didn't rank anywhere near a butler in my mind—Alena, on the other hand... To have a valet such as her in his service, that was no small matter. At any rate, he was right that it was cozier with the fire turned up. The light of the flames, subdued beneath the mantle a moment before, now brightly danced upon our laps and the crystal absinthia on the cart's silver tray. And of the absinthia, I wasn't surprised that an absinthe service would be part of the suite, the drink being a local mainstay, but I have to say, this particular service was among the finest I'd seen: an ice-filled, crystalline absinthe fountain with a glass fairy at its peak, two crystal reservoir glasses, atop of each, a stainless steel absinthe spoon and a resting rectangular cube of whitened sugar, and beside them, the decanted bottle of the fuchsia colored Providence Six absinthe.

Hansen must've found the service as pleasing; he appeared as eager as I to partake. "May I do the preparations?" he asked.

"That would be splendid," I said.

"Excellent. If you could," he said, nodding toward the floor behind the cart. "The entertainment is in that box right there."

He lifted the decanter of fuchsia absinthe from the cart and held it up and away from us so that we could compare it to the nebula beyond the transparent wall. "I'll be," he said. "The same shade."

"I believe that's the point," I said. "To lead you to believe it's a sample of the actual nebula."

"Brilliant," he said, then slowly drizzled the absinthe over the first sugar cube.

I lifted open the lid of the box. Inside, on a bed of red velvet, were two large chrome hoops—I'd guess they were twenty-five centimeters across, no thicker than a heavy gauge wire—and when I removed them, I found them to be incredibly lightweight. I held them up before me, one in each hand, glimmering in the firelight. "And what are these?" I asked.

"They're headsets," he said.

"Headsets?"

"Yes." Having filled the reservoir of the first glass with absinthe, he moved to pour over the next cube of sugar. "The penthouse is equipped with a neural lace interface that will allow us to link into a simulation—a virtual world."

"Really?" I said, placing one of the rings upon my head. "They're far more delicate than any neural interfaces I've seen before."

"Well. We're not traveling far."

"No. I suppose not," I said. I puckered my brow. "Where exactly did you have in mind?"

Having finished pouring the absinthe, he slid each of the glasses into place beneath the two fountain taps, then switched them on. Slowly, cold water began to flow from the taps over the cubes and into the reservoirs, transforming the clear fuchsia absinthe to a pink, milky elixir.

He held out a hand. "May I?" he asked.

"Certainly," I said, handing him his ring.

He fit his headset onto his scalp. The reflection of the fire on the chrome created an illusion of illumination and I was curious if mine looked the same. "Well," he said. "We were just speaking of how, as children, we use to play Hide and Seek."

"We're going back to the yards?"

"Dear, no." He shrugged. "Though that may have also been of some satisfaction. But no. With the aid of our neural lace, we're going to play a new game."

"Oh," I said. "I've done the virtual before. But not direct with the lace, just with the suit and goggles."

"Where did you find an old rig like that?"

"There's a place...it's not important. Anyway. I'm intrigued."

With the sugar now melted and the glasses full, Hansen shut off the fountain's taps and the last trickle of ice water ceased to flow. He offered me a glass, took one for himself, then held his up toward the nebula in the same manner as he had with the bottle. I marveled at the small pink cloud as he twisted the small glass in his hand.

"The common name for the nebula," I said, "is the *Eye of God*, and they say—"

He turned to me with a raise of his brow and the curl of a grin. *"They?"*

"Indeed. *They*," I said. "*They* say that the absinthe allows one to peek inside."

"And what say you?"

"I say," I held up my own glass to clink beside his. "I say, cheers to the quest."

"Indeed," he said, clinking his cocktail to mine. "Cheers."

A brutal anise fire of bitter and sweet filled my mouth.

As I swallowed, the liquid lightning burned my throat, sending a warm quiver cascading down my spine then up again, culminating in a slight full body convulsion and an echoing shudder that set my teeth to chatter.

There was a brief calm, then the electric wave pulsed through me again. My stomach responded with a nauseated revulsion, forcing me to gag, but before I could vomit, the sensation ebbed away; in its place, a warmth of euphoria blanketed me.

"Hrrm," said Hansen, clearing his throat. Softly, he added, "That is quite the elixir."

My eyes going wet with tears, I rasped out a, "Quite."

"Cheers," he said again, holding up his glass. I raised mine. With a slight squeak, I responded, "cheers," then finished off the remainder of my glass.

The second drink was far more soothing.

My shoulders grew soft, and my gums numb. I ran my tongue across the back of my teeth and puckered my lips and cheeks. My mouth felt foreign.

I set my absinthe glass back onto the tray, peered to the fire, and instantly winced. My eyes had become suddenly sensitive to the brilliance of the flames. "Whoa," I said softly. I slid deeper into the chair, rested my head back, and let my lids fall closed.

The neural lace linked quickly.

I was no longer sitting in Hansen's library in front of the fire; rather, I was submerged, surrounded by water. My heart jumped and I gasped. *"Relax,"* said Hansen, but not aloud—only in my head. *"You're still breathing."* And I realized I could breathe; or, at least, that I wasn't suffocating.

The threat of drowning passed; I took in my new environment.

I was floating in an endless, inky blue pool that could have as easily been in a large tank or an ocean. Though there were no visible walls or surface, a pale-pink light fought in from high above.

A loud gurgle rushed close behind me, and I spun in time to see a bearded purple merman accelerate past, his tail slamming up and down, leaving a trio of small bubbling cyclones in his wake as he disappeared into the darkness.

"I'll be," I said, and heard my words in my head as I'd heard Hansen's. *"Is that you?"* I asked.

"I don't know who you're referring to," said Hansen. *"But it wasn't me. I'm somewhere else. You'll have to find me."*

"I see," I said.

"Hide and Seek, remember?"

"So I'm 'It'?"

"Actually, in a sort, we both are," he said. *"We have to find each other."*

"Oh. So it's more Seek."

"I suppose. But we're hidden from each other."

"Do we share clues?" I asked.

"Yes," he said. *"Exactly. You said you just saw someone. Are you in a public place?"*

35

"I'm in the water," I said, *"and I just saw a purple merman swim by. I don't know if it's public, the light is dim."*

"Quite right."

"You're in the water too?"

"No, no. I'm on the surface. No atmosphere. When you gasped, I thought you were too. That's why I reminded you to breathe."

"So how does it work? The game? How do we play?"

"We move toward each other," he said. *"The first step, I'd guess, is for me to find water or you to find land."*

"Providing we're on the same planet."

"I hadn't thought of that. I'm in a small canyon surrounded by a high rock formation."

"Can you see the sky?" I asked.

"It's the nebula. Essentially the same view as the window of the penthouse."

"Then we're most likely near each other."

"You see the nebula too?" he asked.

"No," I said. *"But there's pink light above me. I believe it's coming from the surface."*

"I'll try to find higher ground," said Hansen. *"Can you swim upward?"*

"I don't know," I said. *"I'll try."* I swung my arms before me in an attempt to pull myself forward. *"Amazing,"* I said.

"What is?"

"My fingers. They're webbed."

"It's the construct. It will morph your body to fit your environment. Has anything else changed?"

"Hold on," I said, attempting to right myself. I found that bobbing submerged had a few limitations. For one, when I bent to inspect my feet, I ended up in a somersault, and when I straightened myself back, I flipped the other way. I attempted this a few more times but, though the construct was virtual, fell prey to Newton's third law—for every action I executed, there was an equal and opposite reaction. I spun over so many times that I became dizzy.

Then I decided on a different tact.

Having not succeeded at the many iterations of the maneuver, I waited until I was stabilized then, as gently as I could, simply peeked down past my belly toward my toes.

What I found was a purple scaled, wide finned tail.

Apparently, I was a merman too.

"Amazing," I said again.

"Are your feet webbed too?"

"Something of the sort," I said. *"I think I've figured out what I need to do. And the timing couldn't have be better."*

"Why's that?" Hansen asked.

"I'm not alone down here," I said.

"The merman is back?"

"No. something else."

My visibility was ten meters at best before the inky blue dissipated to black and it was at this shadowy edge of my vision that appeared what at first seemed to be a long, thin line. It ran vertical, an undulating thread, floating closer, taking shape and dimension, until I realized it was not so much a string as the elongated tentacle appendage of something in the darkness beyond.

"What is it?" asked Hansen.

"It's a tentacle," I said. *"Though I'm not quite sure if it's dangling from above or reaching from below."*

"You'd best move away."

My mind was swirling. The nausea returned to my gut. I decided that, unable to see the depths, up was the way out—go for the light and that sort of thing. I placed my arms to my sides, aimed my chin toward the pale-pink, then with the slightest possible effort, moved my toes, or the part of me where toes would be, forward then back then forward again.

The subtle pressure of water pressed onto my face as I moved upward.

"Okay," I said. *"I'm on the move."*

"Good. Me too. Let me know when you reach the surface."

I pressed forward, or upward as the case may have been. As happens beneath the surface, the pale-pink light stayed the same, never seeming to brighten. I told myself that it would open soon and that, having no reference to this virtual sea, I was simply much deeper than I had thought.

"Hansen," I said after a few minutes in, *"I have to say, this portion of the game is becoming monotonous."*

"Don't fret," he said. *"You won't have to go too much farther."*

It was right then that a trail of bubbles rose past me. I watched them as they raced upward, until they faded into the shine of the light.

Then there were more.

I thrashed my tail in an attempt to speed up my ascent. The only sign it was working was that the bubbles' flight slowed.

I bent my head forward. The tentacle was still there, dangling in front of me. Still swimming upward, I let my eyes dart to my peripheral, to the right, to the left. What I found was that the incidents of tentacle had multiplied. In fact, I was surrounded by undulating tentacle strands.

More bubbles rushed past, and I dared to peek down, into the darkness below.

There, barely lit, gently rising beneath me, was the form of a beast.

My heart raced. I kicked franticly, slamming my tail back and forth, in an effort to get away. But it was hopeless. The creature was too large and overtook me as easily as floating upward.

Its tentacles drew close to me and I stopped pushing upward or risked ensnaring myself in its grasp.

"Hansen," I softly said, "I don't like this game anymore."

"Hmm," he said. "I have a confession."

"You don't like it either?"

"I've never liked it. But I thought it was fitting."

"Fitting? But how?"

"It was the game we played as children."

"I want to stop now." I placed my hands to my head but found no chromium band. "How do we stop?"

"You can't," he said.

"What do you mean we can't stop?"

"That's part of the confession. I had Alena add something to the absinthe. A bit of a lock, if you will."

"A lock?"

"The Providence Six Absinthe is a strong distraction, but not strong enough for my intent. I needed to be sure I could anesthetize your body but still have access to your mind."

"Hansen? Why would you do such a thing?"

"Ah, you see, Conrad, that's the other part of the confession. I'm not Hansen."

"Well then. Who are you?" I asked.

"Would you believe, Benny Melker?"

"I don't understand. Melker?"

"Yes. You see the story about driving Hansen to succeed is true. He tracked me down—to rub my face in it, I suppose. Thing is, I was quite happy to see him. When he found me, I was in a bit of financial peril, and he was a convenient remedy *to my ills. Hansen may have been successful in status and station, but he was still weak and easily manipulated. I tricked him into a virtual game of Hide and Seek, then trapped him in the game in order to take possession of his body and fortune."*

"That's criminal," I said. *"You evolved from a bully to a full-blown criminal."*

"Matter of perspective, I guess. You see, from mine, I was the one who was bullied by the rest of the class. Treated as a gnat. Your words, not mine, but equivalent. Now, it was never my intention to be vindictive, to seek revenge. It wasn't until Hansen showed up to gloat that the opportunity presented itself. It was spontaneous, but I have to say that it worked so well, I've repeated the task several times."

"Repeated?" I asked. The tentacles that a moment before had been floating around me began to settle on my flesh, wrapping around me as they did. Tightening.

"With Hansen's fortune, I had a sudden influx of capital, a financial means and, like you, all the time in the world. So I hunted down all of the old classmates, one by one. Attaining their fortunes. Joston, Martin, Riley—each and every one. And Conrad, I plan to do the same to you."

I found myself engulfed, the thin tentacles coiled around me, squeezing. With barely a breath, I exclaimed, *"Melker, you're a monster!"*

"Ha, ha, ha," laughed Melker. *"Conrad, I have another confession. I'm not on the surface. I'm right here with you."*

39

33

Tales from the
CANYONS of
the DAMNED

MOLLY THYNES

JASON LAVELLE

BARRY CHARMAN

TIME FOR A TRIP
PRESENTED BY USA TODAY BESTSELLING AUTHOR
DANIEL ARTHUR SMITH

Auntie_lena314
Molly Thynes

THERE USED TO BE a video channel online. It was called Auntie_lena314. The videos have long since been taken down and even the channel as a whole was blocked.

She posted her first video on May 27th. For the first ten seconds, you saw just a teenage girl with sun bleached hair in a pink cardigan fiddling with the webcam, showing just how inexperienced she was with creating web videos.

"Hello, world! My name is Auntie Lena," she said as she took a seat in the desk chair.

She told the viewers that this wasn't going to be a video channel about boy bands or makeup. Her voice squealing, she told everyone how her nephew, Henry, had just been born yesterday. She created this channel to document the earliest moments of his life.

She was especially excited because her sister, Nan, was going to be moving back home with Henry. She wouldn't be able to keep a baby in the dorms.

"Nan's not too thrilled about moving back home, but at least it's rent-free and she'll have a place to live."

Auntie Lena promised to post a video every few days. She talked about how adorable her nephew was, how she was sure she saw him smile at her. She would film little Henry in the different outfits that relatives sent, chubby and pink with a few strands of almost-red hair. In some of the videos, she appears with dark circles under her eyes,

43

saying little Henry had kept her up all night crying, or he was struggling with a particularly bad bout of colic. But for the most part, they stayed boring little mundane videos in Nan's little room, and the views never climbed above thirty.

Then, on June 13th, she posted a video where she was fidgeting, biting her lip, her hands clenching the seat of her chair. She told the viewers about her sister, Nan. She was refusing to change him or feed him, and for the last three days, she hadn't changed her clothes or brushed her hair.

"I've been doing a lot of reading online," Auntie Lena said, her eyes avoiding the camera. "I think Nan might have postpartum depression. I might not be putting up a new video for a few days, because I want to do some more reading about this."

But on June 16th, things seemed to be getting worse. Auntie Lena started the video by thanking all her viewers for the articles they had sent on postpartum depression.

"But Nan's been getting worse," Auntie Lena said, holding the camera in front of her face as she walked down the hallway.

When Auntie Lena turned the camera around, she was standing in the doorway to Nan's bedroom. In the center of the room, Nan stood with slumped shoulders, dressed in wrinkled, damp pajamas, her hair stringy and oily. As Auntie Lena moved closer to her sister, you could see that Nan was standing over the baby's bassinette.

"Nan?" Auntie Lena asked as she moved to film her sister's face. "Nan, will you say something to me?"

As Nan's face came into profile, you could just make out her lips moving as she looked down at her baby. If you had your headphones on and the volume turned all the way up, you could just barely hear Nan's words.

"Not mine…he's not my baby…how does no one else notice?"

Auntie Lena spent almost a minute trying to get her sister's attention, even shoving the camera right into her sister's face, but Nan didn't so much as look away or tell her sister to leave her alone. Eventually, Auntie Lena gave up and returned to her room. She set the camera back on top of the computer and settled into her chair once again.

"She's been like this for days. I don't mean just the not taking care of herself or Henry. She's saying all these weird things about how

Henry's not her baby. I know that women with postpartum depression say they feel a disconnect from their babies, but this just seems...off."

Reaching off to the side, Auntie Lena grabbed a few sheets of printed paper.

"One of the things I came across in these articles is this thing called postpartum psychosis. Maybe that's what happening, but I don't know. Mom and Dad are trying to get Nan in to see a doctor. I hope it happens soon."

Then, on June 18th, anyone who was awake in the middle of the night saw a...disturbing new upload to Auntie Lena's channel. The video opened to pitch black with Auntie Lena fumbling with the camera, as though she was just waking up and trying to remember how to turn it on.

"Do you hear that?"

In the dark frame, you could just make out the outline of Auntie Lena's face, but this wasn't a camera with a night vision function, so pretty much all you had to go on was the audio. You could hear the *rustle rustle* as Auntie Lena kicked off the sheets and climbed out of bed, the soft sound of her bare feet as she ventured out into the hallway.

Finally, you were able to see some light coming from the crack under a door.

"Nan? Are you up?"

Auntie Lena opened the door and held up the camera to show Nan once again standing over Henry's bassinette. In one hand, she was gripping tight to a box of matches. Then the camera picked up a bright flash of light as Nan struck a match and dangled it over the bassinette.

"DAD!" Auntie Lena shrieked as she leaned out into the hallway. From the furthest door down, a silver-haired man bolted out into the hall, nearly crashing into Auntie Lena.

"Nan, don't!"

Their father rushed into the room, pushing Nan away from the baby, grabbing tight around her wrist until his knuckles turned white. Nan lost her grip on the match, sending it flying towards the curtains. Flames raced along the bottom hem, and climbed upward towards the ceiling.

In the struggle, Auntie Lena rushed into the bathroom, pulling a bucket from under the sink. As she filled it with water, you could hear Nan scream from the other room. "It has to die! It has to be burned!"

Running back to the room, she tossed the camera onto the bed. The frame went sideways, but showed Auntie Lena splashing water onto the fire while Nan struggled with everything she had to get away from her father, who was using the whole of his body weight to keep her pinned to the floor.

"Paul, what's happened?" a woman shouted from outside the frame.

"Janet, call 911!"

Auntie Lena managed to put out the fire and looked back to toward the bed, as though she had just remembered she had left the camera running. Shooting past her father and sister, she reached for the camera and the video came to an end.

Why she even posted a video like that, none of her viewers were able to figure out. The host site did have a function where you could stream live video from your camera directly to the site, so Auntie Lena probably had no idea what she was about to walk into. People were trading different theories back and forth in the comment section of her other videos almost immediately after it happened.

On June 19th, Auntie Lena appeared on camera, white as a bedsheet.

"Nan's gone."

After Auntie Lena had cut off the video footage, the police came to the house. Even in the presence of men with guns, Nan refused to stop fighting or insisting that her baby had to die. It took both of them to force Nan out of the room and out of the house.

"We just got an update this morning."

Nan was being transferred from the jail to a psychiatric hospital. They were trying a bunch of different medications, but Nan would be staying there until the County Attorney decided what to do with her.

On June 25th, little Henry appeared for the first time on camera. Auntie Lena explained that with Nan away, she had to step up and take over a lot of the care of her nephew.

"At least it's summer vacation. Health class was right when they said high school kids aren't meant to raise children."

You see, little Henry was not an easy baby to take care of. He would cry at all hours of the night, and for most of the daytime hours too. He had been difficult to breastfeed, but he wasn't taking to the bottle any better. His skin was loose and it didn't have that baby-soft feel that people went on and on about, and it even seemed to be taking on a blueish grey color. And Auntie Lena was terrified that the baby was going to starve.

On some level, the more Auntie Lena talked about Henry, the easier it was to see how her sister could have lost her mind taking care of him.

On June 27th, Lena appeared on camera with dark circles under her eyes. She was holding her head in her hand, twisting her hair around her fingers.

"I'm wondering…is it possible for babies to go insane? Because I think that's what's happening to Henry."

She said Henry was becoming much more than just a fussy baby. He still cried as much as ever, but the cries themselves had begun taking on an entirely different, more distressing tone. Not the cry of a baby, but…

Auntie Lena listed off everything that reminded her more of Henry's cries. Someone who had had their hand slammed in the door, someone who had a cigar put out on their thigh, a cat having its tail sawed off. The cries of someone who suffered agonizing pain just from existing.

Auntie Lena struggled to detail everything that was happening. She was slumped in her chair, struggling to keep eye contact with the camera. Whenever she did manage to look her viewers in the eyes, you could see the dull luster both her eyes and her skin were taking on.

"What he needs right now is his mom, but Nan isn't going to be coming back for a long time."

For several days, no new videos were posted on Auntie Lena's channel. Instead, she set up a live video feed right in front of Henry's bassinet. On the first night, Auntie Lena got in front of the camera and told the viewers she was going to learn what was happening at night once and for all.

For three nights, nothing happened. Like Auntie Lena said, Henry would cry at all hours of the night. But then on the fourth night, everyone up at three in the morning got to see one of the 'crazy fits' Auntie Lena was talking about. From the slanted angle, you watched Henry shake, just a little bit, then begin screaming the most ungodly scream. It didn't stop there. The baby began convulsing, his head bending backwards, pushing his little chest upward.

Finally, it all ended with a fit so violent, Henry propelled himself out of the bassinet, where he just laid limp and crying until Auntie Lena stumbled into the scene.

After the live feed, Auntie Lena didn't post anything for over a week. And with the view count on her videos skyrocketing, the comments section began piling up.

Make another video, crazy girl.

Fakey fake fake.

When do we get to see the demon baby again?

Then, on July 1st, Auntie Lena appeared on camera once again. For the first several seconds of the video, Auntie Lena did not look at the camera. Her hair was lank, stringy, and unwashed. She was still wearing her pajamas, and from the wrinkles and the stains, she had clearly been wearing them for days.

"Well, you've all seen the livestream of Henry. I've seen it too. I'm…just not sure what it was I saw."

Of course, she told her viewers, she had shown the video of what happened to her parents. Horrified, little Henry was taken straight to the doctor. Every test the tiny county clinic was capable of performing was done on Henry, each of them turning up nothing.

"The doctors actually saw the exact same tape you all saw, but even they don't know what's happening right now."

The family would have to take Henry to a larger hospital two hours away if they wanted any kind of medical answers.

On July 5th, Auntie Lena posted another video in what felt like a much more eerily quiet house. In her more recent videos, no matter how faint, you could usually make out Henry crying from somewhere in the background, or Auntie Lena's parents pacing the halls back and forth, walking him, rocking him, trying to calm him down. But today, it was just Auntie Lena, her and a book with a blue quilted cover she held in her lap as she played with the fringes along the edge.

"Mom and Dad drove Henry out to the hospital yesterday. The doctors want scans of his brain."

Auntie Lena had chosen to stay behind.

"Please don't send me any more messages. I'm not really interested in what strangers think anymore."

Auntie Lena held the quilted book up against her chest. Still bright and brand knew, the tiny details, like the bright yellow ducks or white airplanes, stood out brightly.

"Besides," she said as she opened the book, "I think I have everything I need right here."

Auntie Lena confessed that she had gone snooping through Nan's room and, shoved underneath the mattress, she found the baby book Nan had bought for Henry. Auntie Lena held the book up to the camera. It showed the first photo taken of him at the hospital, the little card that had been on his crib, his hospital bracelet, his little black ink footprints. All the cute little mementos mothers saved after their children were born.

"But here's where it starts getting strange."

She flipped three pages forward, and that's where the actual baby book ended. Instead, the next several pages were filled with writing. Lists, paragraphs, small and large letters filling up the pages from margin to margin. Between that and how Auntie Lena had found it under her sister's mattress, the thing read more like a serial killer manifesto than a baby book. People said as much in the comments.

"Nan wrote all this," Auntie Lena told her viewers. "Let me read some of it to you."

Auntie Lena opened the book. At first, Nan's writing was simply a mirror of what Auntie Lena had been recording in her videos. Henry wouldn't eat; Henry was colicky and fussy. And because of it all, his skin was losing its softness, and his fine little strands of hair were turning sticky and clumping together.

Then came an entry about a horrific nightmare Nan had one night.

"The entire house was on fire. Somehow, I was managing to avoid all the flames, but then I saw Lena stagger from around the corner, completely engulfed. Lena ran for Henry's bassinet. Then she picked him up in her arms while she was still on fire, and he started to shriek as Lena's flames spread to him."

But what was truly terrifying was everything that happened after.

"Even after I woke up, the screams followed me into the waking world. But eventually I realized that the screams were coming from Henry, the sort of sounds a person could only make as the flesh was charred from their bones.

"Since that nightmare, I haven't been able to sleep at night." With all Henry's crying, he never let Nan sleep for more than a few hours at a time anyway.

So instead, Nan would stay up at night, just watching her baby and detailing everything she saw in Henry's little baby book.

She made note of every one of Henry's horrific cries, comparing each one to some horrific pain that could be inflicted on a human being, just as Auntie Lena had done when she first started detailing Henry's disturbing behaviors, before she knew her sister was doing the exact same thing.

Doctors are always so quick to write off a young, hysterical mother.

The rest of what Auntie Lena read were Nan's speculation on just what could be wrong with her baby. It started off with some fairly mundane guesses – *she wasn't feeding him enough, he had some kind of disease from birth that the doctors missed*—gradually becoming more fantastic—*he had picked up some tropical fungus from the gifts from relatives in Florida*—and horrifying—*someone was poisoning him*—on and on and on.

"Eventually, she just starts writing this same word over and over again," Auntie Lena said, finally looking up at the camera. "Changeling."

After that video, Auntie Lena became much more faithful about weekly postings; most weeks, posting two or three. But by now, Auntie Lena had chosen to go in a different creative direction with her channel. Instead of Auntie Lena sitting at her desk in her bedroom, these videos all featured Henry. Gone were the adorable, Facebook-worthy videos, and in their place was something more out of a horror movie. Henry's skin had turned a sickly yellow-grey. His face, his arms, his chest displayed all these crater-like lesions: deep, but none of them were scabbed or bleeding.

In one video, little Henry was on his stomach, laying on the floor, the camera propped up right in front of him. Henry was bawling his same jarring cry. Auntie Lena's feet paced back and forth behind him across the frame. This went on for about thirty seconds until it was just Henry alone in the shot.

And then...*crash!* A glass pitcher dropped to the floor, right in front of the baby. Shards of glass flew through the air, a few across the baby's face, slicing open his left cheek. Blood poured from the cuts, but that wasn't what people reacted to most in the video. It was Henry's silence following, the first silence the viewers had ever seen from the baby. Face still smeared with tears and snot and blood, the baby just stared out at the broken glass, completely transfixed.

That's where the video cut out.

At this point, the comment section exploded with people saying they were reporting her channel, that they were calling the police.

Auntie Lena finally addressed these comments on July 30th. For that video, she went back to her old format of her sitting in her room in front of her computer.

"I've been reading all your comments," Auntie Lena's voice was flat. "You can show these videos to the police, but they probably won't believe any of this is real. Nothing I've filmed is anything a baby should be capable of."

Auntie Lena reached for some wrinkled papers on the desk. "And that's exactly what I wanted to show all of you."

With her one free hand, Auntie Lena shifted the camera left, bringing into view the blue bassinet Henry slept in, in her bedroom.

"Nan suspected and she did her best get the proof." Now Auntie Lena reached for the same baby book she had shown her viewers before. "But I think I finally managed, with these videos, to show that there is absolutely no doubt."

Auntie Lena looked over her shoulder and pointed to the bassinet.

"Henry, the baby you've all been seeing, is not Henry."

Settling back into her seat, Auntie Lena opened the baby book and began flipping through the pages, frantic to the point where she was nearly ripping them.

"In the last parts of Nan's writing, she starts talking a lot about this thing called a changeling," she said. "Babies are taken and replaced with…spirits, demons, or just enchanted objects."

In the background, you could make out the very faintest whimpers and stirring from the bassinet. Auntie Lena ignored them.

"I'm not quite sure when it happened, Nan wasn't really clear on that, but Henry was taken and replaced by that…thing."

Auntie Lena reached over to the side of the desk and held up a stack of wrinkled computer printouts. "Everything I've read says that very often, babies who were disabled or deformed were accused of being changelings, but there are a few ways to know if your baby has truly been taken.

"They cry relentlessly and nothing can console them. Things that normally terrify babies make changelings laugh, or at the very least, stop crying for a few minutes. They are capable of physical feats that human infants are not. And as time passes, they gradually become less and less human-looking."

As if to emphasize this last point, Auntie Lena picked up the camera and carried it over to peer inside the bassinet. Henry lay inside, rasping and jerking unnaturally, like someone on the edges of death.

Auntie Lena turned the camera back to face herself. "There are ways to get rid of a changeling, and some of them even force whoever took your baby to bring it back.

"But…" Auntie Lena looked away, suddenly avoiding eye contact with the camera, "I'm ready to start taking your messages again. If any of you have heard stories about changelings, anything you wouldn't find on the Internet, please tell me. There…aren't a lot of good options I've come across so far."

It was this video that brought all the crazies out. People claiming to be paranormal investigators or cryptozoologists in their comments began listing all the gruesome ways Irish peasants would rid themselves of monsters they thought had replaced their children. That's when Auntie Lena's viewers, who had been there from the beginning, began shouting back.

What the hell do you think you're doing?!?!?!

Have you been watching this girl? She's cray-cray!!!

Stop pushing her! This girl's gonna snap! Don't give her ideas!

Then, Auntie Lena posted what would be her last video.

On July 31st, Auntie Lena set up another special livestream, opening in the family kitchen. As Auntie Lena adjusted the camera, you could see Henry lying behind her. The room was dark, lit only by the streetlamps outside and the bluer light of the moon.

"Thank you all for joining me tonight. Mom and Dad are out…again. To be honest, they really haven't been home much at all lately."

When Auntie Lena moved away from the camera, you could see a large pot on the stove, the kind people used to cook lobster.

"Well, even though it's only been a day, I've received a lot of messages from all of you. But only a few of them were about changelings. Unfortunately, with a few rare exceptions, you don't seem to know much more about changelings than I do."

In the comment section to the right of the video, all of the pervious 'experts' were notably absent. Only Auntie Lena's gathering of loyal followers were there, typing a slow trickle of messages, all repeating different variations of asking her just what was going on.

"There are a lot of ways to find out if there is a changeling in your home, but I've only found two ways of driving one out.

"One is with water, submerging the creature," Auntie Lena said, placing a lid over the large pot. "The other is with fire."

Auntie Lena turned the dial on the gas stove and blue flames shot up from the burner.

"Both are supposed to drive the changeling out of your home," she said, bending down to pick up Henry. "Tonight's going to be a very special episode, because we're going to be testing both at once."

Auntie Lena, with her back to the camera, walked towards the counter. For once, the baby's constant cries had quieted to a few soft whimpers. Auntie Lena bounced him up and down until clear strings of steam rose from up under the lid of the pot on the stove. As the rapid bubbling and busting noises of the boiling water overpowered the hissing of the gas, the comments starting coming through faster and more frantically.

Auntie Lena, what are you doing?!?!

Someone call 911!!!

How?!?! We don't know where she is!!!!!!

Does anyone know how to track the stream?

Lena!!! Don't do something you can't take back!!!!

Auntie Lena lifted the lid from the pot and looked over her shoulder, staring directly into the camera. "You've all seen what I've seen, so you know why I have to do this."

Auntie Lena maneuvered Henry away from her hip, dangling him above the boiling pot. Henry showed no awareness for his surroundings, or of what his aunt was about to do to him; he simply stared blankly out ahead of him, legs hanging limp. Then, Auntie Lena simply dropped him right into the boiling water.

Water splashed and spilled over the stove and onto the countertops, splashing onto Auntie Lena as well. But instead of screaming, like anyone else would have, Auntie Lena slammed the lid of the pot, holding it tightly in place.

The most horrible shrieks you ever heard came from within that pot, which was shaking so violently, Auntie Lena had to stand with the whole of her body weight over the lid just to keep the pot over the burner.

When it finally stopped, Auntie Lena sank to the floor. The previous comments all went dead quiet as silence overtook the kitchen.

Then, Auntie Lena reached into her pocket and pulled out her cellphone.

"Hello...my nephew is dead. No, I haven't checked his pulse or done any of that. Because I know he's dead. Because I burned him in a pot. You should send someone here."

For several moments, Auntie Lena just stared up at the ceiling. Eventually, her head tilted slowly down until her eyes stared directly into the camera.

"I told you all this was going to be a very special episode."

Finally, from outside the view of the camera, came a loud banging on the door. Auntie Lena got up from the floor and picked up the camera.

"Police! Open the door!"

"It's not locked."

The off-screen door flew open and crashed against the wall and two officers—both young men—entered the frame: Officer Regis and Officer Jamison, from the names on their badges.

"Where's the baby?"

The camera turned toward the steaming pot and showed Auntie Lena pointing towards it.

Officer Regis rushed towards the stove, with Officer Jamison right after him, even though there was no chance of saving the baby after it had been boiling for so long.

"I had to do it. We don't have a fireplace and this was the next best thing."

Officer Regis grabbed the pot off the stove with his bare hands and dumped it into the sink, the whole time shouting as the scalding metal burned his hands and the water spattered over his wrists.

Officer Jameson pulled out his flashlight to examine his partner's bright red skin.

The injured officer groaned as the water gurgled down the sink. Clearly, neither of them were listening to Auntie Lena, but still, she continued to explain herself.

"He wasn't a real baby, you see. Whatever it was, we've had it here for weeks, and I spent the whole time trying to figure out what to do with it. I don't know how long it will take to get the real baby back."

"There's no baby here."

"What?" Auntie Lena shrieked, running to the sink, taking the camera with her. Inside, instead of the horror there should have been—boiled flesh—you saw bits of wood, pebbles, and pieces of broken porcelain, the color bleached out of it all by the boiling water.

"Miss," Officer Regis said, his voice pained and his whole body shaking, "where is your nephew?"

"I told you, he's dead and I killed him! He's in that pot!"

Officer Jamison reached for his radio and called out, "We need backup. We have a missing child and a possible EDP."

"Where did he go?" the camera swung back and forth as Auntie Lena searched frantically for whatever it was she had just boiled alive. "Do they just disappear after you burn them?"

"Miss, give me the camera."

Officer Regis reached his blistered hand, with its weeping sores, into view of the camera as he fought Auntie Lena for the device. She fought and screamed, and the camera shook and the audio cracked before it went crashing to the ground.

That's where the video cut out.

The next day, Auntie_lena314 was scrubbed from the host site. I'm sure the police would have been very interested to see what Auntie Lena had been documenting in the first few weeks of her nephew's life, but the host site certainly had good reason not to hand over those recordings which were, essentially, video evidence of a girl slowly going mad and them doing nothing to stop it. But with no actual video, witness statements were worthless.

It also did nothing to tell Auntie Lena's loyal viewers just what happened to her. But if you knew what to type into a search engine, you were still able to follow what happened to her. In rural New York, a fifteen-year-old Lena McCannon was arrested in connection with the disappearance of her nephew, Henry. She insisted she had killed the baby, boiling it alive, but was never able to produce a body. In a hearing, she was deemed incompetent to stand trial. She now resides in the same psychiatric hospital as her sister, Nan, until such time as she is deemed fit to proceed.

The Rockland county sheriff's office asks that anyone who has any information about the whereabouts of Henry McCannon to please contact them.

A Wonder Made of Skulls
Barry Charman

IT WASN'T CLEAR AT what point time travel became less about the destination and more about the journey.

Judd reread the line, expecting something to reveal itself, but it was just too glib. The brochure was so glossy it came with a migraine warning. He wanted to put it away, but he was trying to get into the mood.

That made him think. At what point had time travellers had to *get in the mood?*

They were trying to make you feel important when you were about to be dwarfed by your unimportance. It didn't work. He put the magazine away and closed his eyes, thinking about all the things it didn't tell you.

Someone had to go and break the speed of thought.

They'd *called* it a breakthrough, then gone on to break through whatever else they could find. There were straightforward advances to begin with, then the achievements became more and more radical. Even so, no one had expected to break through *time*. It was an inspired accident, an innovative mistake. But things tend to get out of control when they're not planned.

All too quickly, time had been unravelled. It was divided up, mapped and auctioned off, becoming a commodity, an amusement. *The past is a foreign country, they do things differently there*; and a time traveller's favourite past-time was to go walk in the past, pointing and laughing at *foreigners*. What was stated first as a philosophical observation quickly became an advertising legend.

This activity had kept Judd busy for ten thousand years. Well, ten thousand years had kept him busy for the best of one. His desk job had started to get claustrophobic when the small print began dancing. They'd told him to take a break, go off and take a time-out. He remembered how Leonard had slapped him on the back, told him to go "pick the Sphinx's nose."

He squeezed the pads implanted beneath his fingers, called up a time door, and walked though, careful as always to lock it behind him. He emerged back in the deep past.

Great. *The Dinobores*. Judd smiled thinly; the height of technology was the act of yawning at a dinosaur.

There was an old saying: *Don't close the brackets*. In travellers' parlance, this meant: be wary of excessive time travel. Don't go too far back or too far ahead. The mind might not accept what it sees. Keep the possibilities open, allow time to *breathe*. Judd had gone prehistoric before; he'd taken the tour to the mud pits, taken pictures as an ancestor had half drowned on dry land. *A confusing spectacle,* they called it. *Fifty credits! Get your picture taken by one of our official guides!*

What a waste.

He only came back because it reminded him of Becky. She'd loved being *scared,* would grab his arm then laugh at herself. Odd, the things one remembered.

There was nothing more desolate than a glimpse of man's raw beginnings. Few did the tour twice. Same for the future. Half of Europe is a road of skulls, and no one wants to know why. A vision you can't change is a terrible thing.

Judd walked over to a rock and sat; he watched a Diplodocus as it walked in the distance towards some trees. He instinctively lifted a finger to the side of his head. One tap would activate the camera attached to his cornea. A nice picture for the folks back home. Subtle. Non-intrusive. Dull.

He lowered the hand, then turned to look back at his footprints. Walking backwards, they stopped abruptly with no indication to their origin. The door was gone for now, waiting to be called.

Judd sighed. Somewhere, he'd lost the magic. He remembered his first tour, that tight panic he'd felt when he'd turned and saw the door gone.

He got up and took a walk, wondering *when* he could go from here.

Rome? There was a great tour he'd heard about. He could toast marshmallows in the fire as the city burnt. They made it *fun*. He'd heard about their last tour, where they'd had a contest seeing who could tickle Schopenhauer first.

Mind you, it *was* getting a bit reckless. It had all been so solemn once, almost anxiously over-regulated. But slowly, over time, the tours had become more flexible. Of course, there were always some people saying they were on the verge of vandalism. But if you didn't make history interactive, then what was it? A pantomime parade of the dead.

The politicians had nightmares at first—about governments undoing each other and rewriting history—but the regulations had been strict enough to convince everyone. Even the religions had backed it up.

Create the doors, they'd said, *go through.*

He wondered what it was they'd expected to find. Had they given their endorsement expecting to find endorsement in turn? In the stirring of the past? If so, they hadn't got lucky. Faith hadn't endured time travel; it hadn't survived the *revelation.*

Judd had gotten a few laughs out of that. He'd replayed over and over the holo-discs of the priests who'd gone on one of the early tours; loving the looks of disappointment on their faces when they returned. Turned out religion had raised questions science could permanently answer. They'd always felt *special,* with the imaginary voice in their heads filling them up with hollow justifications for their every sin. Now, they were the same as everyone else.

Even now, Judd took some satisfaction at the memory. No one had ever made *him* feel special. His parents had preferred divorce over keeping the family together; mum had taken his brother but not *him.* She'd established a pattern. There should have been a girl waiting for him back home, but she'd moved on to someone else. The last time he'd seen her she'd dyed her silver hair blond, told him she was going off to marry someone in Paris in 1945. They'd picked out a nice spot, just after the war. They were going to set up a tasteless vineyard called *Hope's Fruit.* Hell, even his promotion had found someone else—

Judd paused and released a heavy sigh. He needed to remember why he'd taken this time off. His life had been closing in around him— constricting him, overwhelming him with the sheer banality of existing.

Tired, he called up a door.

Judd walked through, locked it, then looked around. He was on the *Marie Celeste*; they ran a neat tour. Usually threw a good boat party, at least.

The boat was deserted.

That's weird, he thought.

Wandering around the deck, Judd looked inside the cabins and down in the bunks. No one. There was always *someone* on the *Marie Celeste.*

There were just sounds that creaked in the wind and shadows that danced with the dust.

As the sun went down, Judd summoned another door and walked though.

Ah, Jerusalem. It always amused him that the Bible had evolved into just another brochure. Walking towards a narrow, winding road, he listened to the sounds of a distant market. It was dusk, and the sun here was also setting. The evening was mild, a soft breeze made him feel welcome.

There was a creak behind him.

Judd turned, frowning. The door was open. It should have disappeared as soon as he'd locked it—

Oh.

He winced. That was careless. If anyone had *seen...*

He walked back to the door and locked it. It vanished like a promise made in a dream.

As Judd was about to walk on, he looked down at his footprints.

Two pairs.

He remembered where he was and smiled wryly. Even so, the image was unsettling. He thought back to the *Marie Celeste.*

They had to lock the doors. Not just to keep the time periods sealed off, not just because you didn't want "foreigners" crossing the borders (which in itself was a parody of any period you visited), but also because of the *unknown.*

The *"what if"* as they called it back home.

What if there was something between the doors? And what if they forgot to *lock* the doors, and what if that something *noticed...*

Nonsense. The unnerved thoughts of people cowed by progress.

Still. They had broken the speed of thought, which *had* enabled them to open doors onto all of time and step through. You had to treat this stuff with some respect. He briefly thought of all the scare stories their scientists had flagged up. He'd only skimmed them, personally. It had all seemed so alarmist, so *feeble*.

They'd talked like time was a thread you could pull apart at any second. Before his first tour, there'd been a brief lecture on *unimaginable perversions*. That had been a popular phrase of theirs. Like they couldn't even predict how things could get messed up. Great bit of science, that.

Judd stared at the prints a little longer, then tried to shake off the feeling that was beginning to shadow him.

He checked his guide for the nearest meeting point, then activated his projector. Immediately, his clothing shimmered and he was disguised in the local attire. *Always blend in,* he thought, *and always lock your doors.*

Hurrying now, he made his way to the tour point: an innocuous grid reference that should have been bustling with tourists, each of them shimmering with an aura only an enhanced eye could detect. But there was no one there. He gazed around, expecting some tech to start giving him signals, but nothing happened. Just as Judd began to wonder what had happened to everyone, a door opened nearby. Surprised by how relieved he felt, he waited for someone to step through.

He waited.

When no one emerged, he approached the door, suddenly nervous. Everything beyond was dark. That meant nothing; it was a door, after all, not a window. Judd wanted to step through; even if it didn't take him home, he might come across a tour group. But why had no one appeared? Why had they left the way open like this?

What if he went through, and home had...altered?

Judd shut down those thoughts, appalled. He closed the door, and it vanished. Increasingly agitated, he ran into the humid night, checking his guide for the next tour point. Despite himself, he began to worry. The rumours began running through his mind again. The theories. They had made doors out of air. They had unwound the unknown. They had opened themselves up to new ideas, new possibilities.

What if they... had *become* doors?

What would that even mean? All of a sudden, Judd wanted nothing more than to be back behind his desk. Sure, life was small, trivial, but what the hell was the opposite? He shouldn't be here, scurrying about in some dim corner of the dark ages. His office was bland and dull and safe; he could feel it smirking at him from across time.

Something knocked. Someone answered.

That thought was wild, yet startlingly clear. As they had broken, could they *be* broken? What did that *mean*?

He saw a key in a lock, imagined entrance as a transference, a corruption, but had no means to shape or complete these thoughts. Stumbling as he went, he thought of that road of skulls and wondered where the first was laid, or the last.

"A mind is a terrible thing to taste..."

Judd stopped in the street. He shivered, feeling totally abandoned and adrift. In the silence, a distant animal howled. The wind coiled and moaned.

"Corrupted. Blind. Witless. Corruption follows. We are crawling over the back of time."

He tried not to panic. Just keep moving, he thought, on to the next door, and the next, and the next—

"Early, this. Malleable. Weapons will be made here. Prophets. Words will become mutilations."

Something was curling around his mind. An intimate sensation, wrong, unnatural. Judd felt disoriented. Suddenly, he remembered those early lectures, about *unimaginable perversions,* and all the rest. *Time travel is a wonder made of skulls.* That was a phrase he'd forgotten 'til now.

"Yes. Yes, it is."

He reached for a concept that he was unable to entirely grasp. Some fear thrown away in one debate or another, that science and religion could both be tools, one used to create the other, both used as fuel to tear everything else apart—

"We will begin here. Poor boy. So sad. So alone..."

Judd hurried into the night, followed closely by two pairs of footprints, the pervading sense of thoughtlessness that he'd brought with him, and a low voice that had begun to fester in his shadow.

A voice that told him he was *special.*

Masks
Jason LaVelle

THE ARTIST LOOKED DOWN at the subject, very pleased with what they had to work with. Though still and pale, the man's face had lost none of the appeal it held in life. A handsome face with hard jaw lines, a straight, prominent nose, and a smooth, not too long, not too shallow brow. The face was easily recognizable, a famous man especially in literary circles, one of the great fiction authors of the last decade. That was one thing death could never take from him: his achievements. And, of course, it could not take his face.

The artist began at his forehead, smearing thick alginate over the face, coating it gently but thoroughly, taking extra care to massage the thick white paste down into the hollows of his eyes so as to lose no detail. The artist's hands moved quickly, scooping more paste then smoothing it, thickening the coat and leaving only two small holes where the nostrils had been. With the man covered from hairline to chin, the artist massaged over the gooey paste once more, feeling and dispelling tiny air bubbles locked within. The alginate set quickly, only three minutes after mixing, and the artist hurried to place thin strips of burlap over the lumpy mask, strengthening the gelatinous mold.

A stack of six-inch strips of plaster bandages lay next to the body, and the artist, using hands clad with blue nitrile, dipped the strips in warm water, squeezed them out, and layered the bandages over the hardening alginate. After placing the last piece of plaster bandage in a bowtie shape connecting the bridge of the nose to the lips, the artist stepped back, admiring the work.

Better. The artist nodded triumphantly. Each mold formed faster, more easily, and with greater detail. *Perfect.* The plaster wouldn't be ready to work with for another thirty minutes, which left time for the artist to clean up the actual scene of the crime.

Jessica set the newspaper down on her kitchen counter, but the face of Ernie Stalward stared up at her. She spooned oatmeal into her mouth, wincing as she caught a spoonful that didn't have sugar on it.

Body Found in Lake Macatawa; Renowned Author Ernie Stalward Dead.

She touched the paper, rubbing her fingers across the newsprint until they came away black. It was a wonder they still made these things, and more of a wonder that she subscribed to it. She lifted her fingers to her nose and drew in a gentle breath, savoring the smell of newsprint and paper.

She'd always preferred the printed word, and in a world of tablets and computers, that made her an oddity, a minority even. Jess let out a sigh and scraped the last of her oatmeal from the bowl. She wasn't shocked by the headline, but it gave her a chill just the same. Stalward was one of five notable authors recently killed in a series of murders that was absolutely astounding the press and media. "Serial Novelists Killed by Serial Killer," the headlines read, or things along those lines.

Jessica remembered the first death well, and the headline accompanying it. "Horror Aficionado Daniel A. Smith Killed by His Obsession." It was a ridiculous headline, in her opinion.

Smith had been killed and his body left in the deep north woods of New York, eviscerated and propped up against a tree. The search party reported that coyotes had eaten most of his 'fleshy' parts. There was no evidence that he knew his attacker, nor that his publishing business had anything to do with his death, but his fondness for the terrible and macabre encouraged the papers make colorful headlines that would have, in other circumstances, been laughed at. Ridiculous though they may be, it gave Jessica an eerie feeling, looking at the names of people she knew in such context.

Jess opened her daytime planner and flipped to the last pages. *Ernie Stalward, Interview* was written in red on last Wednesday's spot. Jess had been so happy to hear Stalward was taking interviews once again. For a freelance journalist, he was a big score.

Stalward had recently released "Doctor Love," a crime drama centered around a philanthropic doctor whose family and friends had no idea he was also using and murdering prostitutes. *A modern day Jack The Ripper* was how Jess had described it in her article. The piece was good; Stalward had been open and funny, even revealing, giving her readers a chance to see beyond the multimillionaire author and look at the mind of a man who had created great fiction.

The article hadn't even been printed when the police found Stalward's body, but Jess suspected this may expedite the process. "Ernie Stalward's Final Review," is what they would call it, or something like that. She leaned back against her barstool. She supposed it was a nice note to go out on, that interview; she'd been quite complementary. Jess tapped her fingers on the countertops. In the last six months, she had interviewed each of the authors who turned up dead. *I'm going to get a reputation for this. Almost like a priest,* she thought, *hearing their last confessions before they met their ends.*

The artist broke away the plaster mold, peeling it bit by brittle bit from the casting. When the alginate finally released, the mold broke free and the plaster *thunked* onto the table. The artist picked it up, holding the oval shaped stone and admiring it: Ernie Stalward's face, cast perfectly in light-grey gypsum. It was beautiful, the most successful death mask yet.

Using a fine dental pick, the artist gently skimmed the stone's surface, smoothing out tiny imperfections around the eyebrows and chipping away the excess plaster from Stalward's nostrils. The artist made one final pass with only gloved fingers, relying on touch to find any hidden burs. There were none. The face was a mask of perfection; perfection cast in stone.

"So beautiful," the artist breathed, holding Stalward's face close to their own. For a moment, the artist swayed on shaky legs, and tears fell from their face.

"Deep breaths," the artist said and gently replaced the mask on the table. Once the tremble settled out of the artist's hands, they came to rest on Stalward's face again, gently massaging the cheeks, then the bridge of the nose.

On the back of the mask, sunk into the plaster, was a thick wall anchor. The artist wiggled the anchor, making sure it was secure and that no cracks would appear, then brought the mask into the study. A sacred air, no less so than that of a church, filled the artist's study. Books and paintings adorned every surface in the room, but the real prizes hung on the wall above the antique hemlock desk. Four exquisite stone masks stared out into eternity, their noble features preserved in perfect detail with a stone plaster. In this room, the legends lived; in this place, they were immortals.

Ernie Stalward's face took its place on the wall next to Artie Cabrera, whose long, soft visage and slightly opened mouth reminded the artist of the monoliths on Easter Island. Compared to Artie, a loud, boastful science-fiction author, Stalward's face was refined, sophisticated, and spoke of a completely different personality. His features were those of an athlete-intellect, a man who, while writing the most gripping crime dramas of their lifetime had also become a para-Olympic triathlete, using his one leg not as a crutch, but as a platform to elevate all those who had been born differently. Ernie Stalward, a great man, now forever a part of this room and its famous inhabitants. The heaviness of the space grew overwhelming, and the artist was forced to retreat, promising the faces a swift return. All things had to be taken in turn and with patience.

The budget was stretched thin, and her publisher was already incensed by the rising cost of airline fuel, but in the end the promise of the interview won them over. Jessica's contact inside the New Queensland Literary group had leaked to her that Sean Brandis was in the United States. The reclusive Brandis, hailing from the great Down Under, never toured, never interviewed, never appeared in the media in any fashion. In fact, it had been rumored that even the photo on his book jackets was fake.

"Dark Meat"—his epic tale of one aboriginal's journey through life in a racist and separatist Australia to find peace and meaning in a culture that had been raped and dismantled by white colonist—was hailed as the greatest piece of Australian literary fiction in the past century. He was a treasure amongst aussies, even though his book was a scathing reprisal to the mostly white continent. "The Australian Herman Hesse," they called him. And he was here.

Jessica had been on her email and her phone all morning, checking, confirming, then rechecking. It was true. Her very last call was to the owner of the Air B&B condo Brandis had rented in Panama City beach. Only after she promised cash and internet notoriety did they divulge that he was indeed hosting Brandis in his house.

"This is it," she told the magazine, "the biggest interview of my life, and probably the best article you'll ever get."

Well, things like that never went over well. *Literary Face* had been in business for many years and had employed not only dozens of talented journalists, but they'd published articles on the biggest authors and screenwriters in the world.

"None like this though," Jess had argued. "This is going to be like unmasking Daft Punk or revealing the true creator of the Bible."

Okay, so maybe she was being a little overdramatic, but she wanted this. Bad. Five years of writing non-fiction articles and the occasional short story had left her with solid freelancing credentials and a reputation for being straight to the point but elegant in a way non-fiction almost never was. "Jessica Perth, the Joan Didion of our generation," she liked to fantasize.

So, stumbling out of the shower naked and dripping all over her tile floor, Jessica leapt for the phone on her counter to see the message thumbnail: *Flight Booked, make it good.*

"Yes!" she screamed, then slipped and cracked her ass on the hard tile in her kitchen. Goddam if this wasn't undignified, naked in a pool of still soapy water. Who knew where her phone flew off to when she fell, probably under the stove. She didn't care. She'd done it; she was going to meet the man with no face.

Florida had been napping quietly under a blanket of humidity when Jessica arrived. At 5:30 p.m., and by the time she tucked her suitcase in the trunk and buckled into her rental car, she was already soaked in perspiration. A Midwesterner by birth, humidity was not an unknown, but the thickness of it took her breath away. Each step felt heavy, and her clothes clung to her uncomfortably. Her toes, tucked neatly into thirty-dollar flats, were slimy and hot.

As she drove, Jessica mentally prepared for her assault on the Australian author. It would be a surprise attack, no warning, and that was usually the best kind. However, she'd had more than one door slammed in her face, and she couldn't let that happen today. That was the sticking part, getting in the door. Once she had Brandis in front of her, Jessica knew she could deliver the interview of a lifetime. But she had to get in.

Waterfront condos flew by outside her window. In the gaps between buildings, Jessica could see the ocean, sparkling and blue-green, an endless expanse of water extending far beyond the horizon. The GPS alerted her, and Jessica looked ahead 500 feet, where a two-story condominium building with grey sides and blue trim rested quietly off the road, watching the water. *Unassuming,* she thought. *Very smart.*

The driveway held a Range Rover and a bright blue moped. The garage door was down and the drapes were drawn. Jessica frowned as she slowed outside the building. Then she cleared the side of another structure and saw the tall fence behind the condo. She slowed further. A swimming pool with people in it.

A loud screech sounded behind her, and the blaring of a horn. Jessica looked into the rearview mirror just moments before a red pickup truck overtook her. She jammed on the gas and braced for impact, jerking the wheel as she did. Her tiny rental squawked and jumped the curb, leapt over a small patch of dry grass, and ground to a stop off the road. Her heart thudded loudly in her ears. Her hands trembled and she flipped the shifter up into park. Then she hugged her chest, rocking gently against her seat as her vision swam and surfaced then dove once more.

Then her door was yanked open. Jessica jumped back in her seat, wide eyed.

"What the fuck is your problem?" A bald man with a red face and a light blue polo top leaned into the car, jamming his finger in her direction.

Jessica couldn't respond, couldn't think. In fact, she could hardly breathe.

"You dumb bitch, you almost fucked up my truck! What the fuck were you stopped in the middle of the road for, you dumbass?"

"I—I, uh," as a writer, she'd never run out of words, until now.

"Get your ass out here, you stupid bitch! Are you drunk or something? Get out here!" The man reached in for her. Sweat dripped off his long nose onto her pants.

"Ey!"

The man looked up as another male voice shouted over to them. Jessica saw the man approaching through the windshield. He walked with a calm swagger, each step a little exaggerated, and though his limbs moved slowly, the man covered ground quickly. A Caucasian male, his thick brown hair was wet and matted on his head. He had a full beard, a mess of riotous curls that dripped off his cheeks and down his neck. His chest was bare and pink with sun exposure. He wore board shorts that stopped at his knees, shorts adorned with blue dolphins jumping through teal waves.

"Whacha doin' there, mate?" the man called. Though he wasn't shouting, his voice carried easily.

Her would-be attacker withdrew from her car and rose to meet the newcomer.

"This bitch nearly ran me off the road."

"How 'bout you cool down a bit, eh?"

"Why don't you go back to where you came from, moron! This isn't your business!"

The man came to stand right next to the car, only a yard away from the red-faced man with the pickup truck.

"I'm afraid that it is. See, she crash-landed here in my driveway, so the way I see it, is she's my responsibility now."

Jessica looked around and saw she'd landed right in the lot she had been stalking; her car had come to a stop only inches away from the little blue moped. *Holy shit*, she thought. *This is him. This is Brandis.*

"Your responsibility? Then you want to take responsibility for what she's done? To my truck?" The red-faced man was somehow turning more red.

Brandis looked around and spotted the truck. "Your truck looks fine to me, mate. Why don't you just drop it?"

The man huffed. "I took about an inch off my new tires trying not to hit her. Now who's going to pay for that?"

Brandis nodded, his beard dancing in a hypnotic way in the hot breeze.

"So, your tires and brakes did what they were supposed to do, right? That's their job, to stop you in case of an accident? Well, then good on them. The way I see it, you should walk away just happy you got them new tires on in time to save your big ass."

The man didn't know how to respond, so he did what all angry men do. He extended a finger and jabbed it at Brandis. The bearded man, who was neither large nor muscular, caught the man's hand and twisted inward. Jessica flinched as suddenly the red-faced man was on his knees in front of Brandis. Brandis spoke in a lower voice, but maintained his cool demeanor.

Jessica strained to hear.

"Now, you can take those new tires and shove them right up your bloody cunt. You stop acting like a prissy bitch and get your fat ass outta here right now before I break your jimmy-yanker. You understand that, mate?"

There was a tense stalemate. Well, tense for the red-faced man. Brandis looked as calm as he had when he'd first strolled into the situation.

"What's that mate?" he asked.

The man mumbled something and Brandis released him. The red-faced man looked over to Jessica once more before shaking his head and walking away, rubbing his wrist as he did so. Brandis watched him go, then came around to her door and peeked inside.

"You all right in there, miss?"

Jessica nodded. Though it was carpeted in thick brown beard, his face was kind and his hazel eyes glimmered from under thick eyebrows.

"You wanna come out? Have a glass of water? Or a beer?"

She hesitated. Here she was, exactly where she wanted to be. *Suck it up and go!* her mind shouted at her. Jessica nodded. "Yeah, that would be nice."

She accepted Brandis's hand when he extended it to her. The ground was shaky beneath her, and she wobbled a little.

"Hey there, easy does it," Brandis said, looping an arm around her. "Let me walk with you, all right?"

"Okay," she mumbled. She let Brandis lead her to the condo and in through the front door.

The house was nicely furnished but poorly lit, giving the space a moody appearance. The brightest light in the place shone in through the slider off the dining room, where the afternoon sun made its slow dance toward the ocean.

"Nice place," she said.

"Thanks, love. It's just a rental, though. I'm from out of town," he said, then gave a chuckle, as if it wasn't obvious he wasn't from there—his accent was unmistakable.

"Here," he said, motioning to a tan microfiber sofa. "Rest your feet for a minute and I'll get you a drink."

The artist packed the suitcase. The case was a hard-sided Samsonite, and not cheap, but good quality items rarely are. Certain necessities went in first: a white smock, blue scrub pants, two-dozen rubber gloves. Three plastic mixing spatulas went in, and a yard of folded burlap. The case still had plenty of room. The artist eyeballed a bag of alginate powder, the paste-like mix which was applied to the subject first that would capture the fine details of their face. *It should be plenty,* the artist decided and carefully set it in the suitcase, then added a long stack of plaster bandages wrapped in cellophane. The last item was a ten-pound bag of ultra-cal 30, the plaster powder that would make up the meat of the death mask. As an afterthought, the artist threw in a change of socks and underwear, along with a short, ironwood dowel with a length of heavy cord. A well-practiced routine, but even still the artist had to work to keep calm and be thorough. The prospect of a new subject always invigorated them, but vigor invited mistakes, and the precise nature of the art was most important. Some say that art imitates life, and some the opposite, but in this case, and not so humbly, the artist felt that their work created not only life but immortality.

"So, you're an artist then?" Jessica asked, her feet curled beneath her on the sofa and a tall glass bottle of beer in her hands.

Brandis laid a towel out on the loveseat opposite her and sat down. His belly pooched out slightly as he sat. He punched at his phone several times then set it on the couch next to him.

"I guess you could say that," he said, and pulled on his beer. "I write books."

Jessica nodded. "That's cool, anything I might know?"

"Well, do you read?"

"I do."

"Then you might know it."

Jessica sighed and rolled her eyes. "Come on, spill it. What do you write?"

"Have you heard of 'Dark Meat'?"

Jessica waited for what she hoped was an appropriate amount of time, then widened her eyes. "You're kidding! You wrote 'Dark Meat'? I love that book!"

Brandis raised his eyebrows at her and pulled on the beer again.

"Wow, I can't believe that's you. Didn't that book win a bunch of awards?"

Brandis shrugged. "Shite, if you ask me. I was in college when I wrote it, bored with class, so I did it to entertain myself. It was all bullshit, though, just fiction."

Jessica shook her head. "How can you call it bullshit? 'Dark Meat' was incredible, and so influential. It changed the way I thought about Australia."

"Eh. It was only incredible and everything because most people don't know shite about Australia. I mean, no offense miss, but do you know anything about Australia besides what was in that book?"

"I guess not. I used to watch The Crocodile Hunter a lot."

Brandis laughed so hard, he spat foam down his beard."

"The Crocodile Hunter? Oh, come on! Ha! But that's what I'm talking about. Nobody knows what really happens out back, so none of you know if the book was total shite or not."

Jessica thought about that for a minute while she drank. This interview was not going the way she planned—it was even better.

"So how do you explain all the awards, the success? Don't you think that if the book was shit that people would have called you out on it?"

"See, that's the funny thing about people, isn't it? They move in herds, just like cattle. A few people start talking about something they like, and pretty soon everyone else jumps on board with 'em." Brandis leaned forward so that the light of the room shone into his eyes. He looked...intense. "I wrote a story about a boy who had a shit life and was always trying to figure out what the hell he was supposed to do."

"No, it was way more than that, it wasn't just about a boy. It was about an entire culture, one that was ransacked. You're undervaluing the book now."

Brandis leaned back and shook his head. "You want me to tell you a secret about that book?"

Oh god yes!

"Yeah, sure."

"Well, when I first wrote it, the story was about me."

Jessica had to fight to keep her jaw from dropping as she stared at the man.

"The story about the dark-skinned aboriginal boy fighting his way through a tormented life was about you?"

Brandis smirked. "Yes ma'am. I only made him an aboriginal when my writing proff told me the story lacked any societal value. I figured the aboriginal angle would make it more—sympathetic, I guess."

Holy shit.

"That's our secret, though, got it?" Brandis said. "I get you out of your car trouble and you keep my secret. Fair enough?"

Jessica nodded. *Gold. Pure gold.*

"Wow, I feel like you've just blown my mind." Jessica's body was practically humming with excitement. And need.

"It's funny meeting you like this, you having read my book and all," Brandis said. His face was round beneath his beard, and a new curiosity crept into his eyes. "So, what brought you to Florida anyway? How did you end up in my driveway?"

Uh-oh.

A knock on the door saved her.

Jessica startled and stood.

"No worries, love, that's just my mate, Jon."

"Jon—"

"Yeah, you'll love him, he's a writer too."

Jessica bristled with that feeling, that strange lust, that uncertain something between excitement and need.

Brandis whipped open the door and was nearly flattened by a man who seemed impossibly large. The man caught Brandis with both arms and the Australian author was swallowed by his hug, disappearing for a moment behind the man's hairy arms.

"Christ, Phrater, you daft cunt, did you manage to get bigger?" Brandis gasped from within the man's grip.

Brandis was released and the big man slapped him on the bicep. "If you weren't such a little pussy, you could take it! Aren't you eating at all out there?"

Then the pair seemed to notice Jessica at the same time and stared in her direction.

Jess raised her eyebrows at them.

"Quite the bromance you've got there," she said. "So, is this an author thing, or are you guys just a little hot for each other?"

Brandis laughed, and she could swear the laughter came out with a thick Australian accent.

"Jon Phrater, this is Jessica—I'm sorry, love, I don't know your last name."

She rose to meet the big man. "I'm Jessica Perth," she said, and extended her hand.

73

Jon grinned at her, a grin that turned into a wide, large-toothed smile. His hand engulfed hers. "I'm pleased to meet you, Jessica." He spoke with a New York accent and pumped her hand twice.

Jon looked back at Brandis. "Where did you find her?"

Brandis eyed her curiously again. "Well, she just kinda got dumped into my lap. But I'm not sorry she did."

Jon still held her hand. The big man was hot and a little sweaty, and Jess felt her own hand beginning to perspire as well.

"Good find, Sean, good find." Jon finally released her hand.

"I hear you're a writer too?" Jess said.

"You've been telling stories, eh, Sean?"

Brandis chuckled. "Come on, let's have a beer."

"Let's do that, but I want to sit next to Miss Perth."

"Jesus, you're creeping her out, you fat American idiot."

"Oh come on, you sound like the spawn of a hillbilly and a British whore. I If anybody's creeping her out, it's you."

Jon was still staring at her, still smiling. He had a strange light in his eyes, a glimmer—no, more like a shimmer, like the shine of a river in the moonlight, slippery, smooth, never-ending.

Deep breaths, Jess, deep breaths. Sean Effing Brandis, and Jon—Prince of Sci-Fi—Phrater. This trip had gone from gold to platinum.

"Boys, nobody is creeping me out, but I need you to excuse me for a minute. I want to go grab something out of my bag in the car."

Jon faltered, and Brandis gave her a look that clearly said no.

"I promise, I'll be right back."

Jon looked to Brandis and the bearded man gave a thin tip of his head. Phrater sighed and made an obvious attempt to freshen his smile.

Jessica shook as she opened the trunk of her rental. She grabbed the handle of her large suitcase, started to lift, then dropped it back into the trunk-well. She reached for the trunk again, and her slender hands shook so fast in the Florida heat that they looked like a mirage.

"Come on, honey, you've got this," she whispered. The biggest opportunity in her life lay before her, and here she stood, shaking like a frightened fifteen-year-old before her first school dance. *I had every reason to be frightened, and look how that dance turned out.* Jessica blew out a deep breath and snapped open the suitcase. She rummaged through the contents for a moment, slipped several items into her pockets, then finally withdrew from the trunk.

The two men were waiting for her in the living room, and they both visibly relaxed when she stepped back through the door. Jessica smiled as she walked into the room.

"You're in my spot," she said, approaching Jon.

The large man smiled wide again and patted his leg.

"Why don't you come sit on Papa Jon's lap?"

Brandis rolled his eyes, but smirked.

"Are you supposed to be Santa Claus now, in the off-season?" Jess asked. One hand slipped into her pocket and started fiddling with the things from her bag.

Jon's laugh was deep and meaty, then he slid over, allowing about twelve inches on the cushion next to him.

Jessica squeezed into the spot then grabbed her beer off the end table next to her and drained the last of it. That steady energy was rising in her again. Anticipation, excitement, desire.

Brandis shifted around in his seat.

"So, you ever got to talk to a famous author before?" Jon asked, leaning too close to her.

"Can't say I have," Jessica answered, glancing over at Jon then looking down into her beer bottle.

"Pretty cool, isn't it?"

"I suppose. You're *friendlier* than I would have thought."

"You've heard of me then?" Jon asked.

"Well, I've heard of *him*," Jessica answered, motioning to Brandis, who burst out laughing.

She looked back at Jon, who was still staring at her. His smile had faded into a grin, but there wasn't any mirth in it.

Jon was breathing heavily, and she got the impression that he was trying to smell her. Jon Phrater, she determined, was a bit of a creep.

"I'm going to hit the pisser," Brandis said and left the room.

As soon as he disappeared down the hall, Phrater leaned closer.

Jessica leaned away, but the big man pulled her face toward him.

"It's okay to be nervous," he said, then put his mouth over hers.

Not the interview she had envisioned. Phrater obviously had one thing on his mind, and there was no getting through to men once they had *that* in their heads. The kiss was slimy and hot, and Jessica thought there could be no better time than this. She withdrew the cord from her pocket, and while Phrater explored her mouth, she looped the cord up and around his neck, then back down again. Phrater paused.

"What are you—"

Jessica gripped both ends of the cord, pulled her knees up to her chest, then kicked out against him with all her strength. Phrater's body jerked back but his head and neck snapped forward.

She reamed on the cord. His face turned red, spittle formed on his lips, and he tried and failed to sputter out some complaint. The cord burned her hands but Jessica pulled harder, pistoning out with her legs as she did. Phrater's eyes bulged from his head, and just when she thought they would burst right out of their sockets, she heard a muffled *crack* and his body went limp, falling on top of her.

Jessica desperately needed a minute to rest, but she didn't have time. She squeezed out from under Phrater's soft body and hurried down the hall after Brandis.

"Argh!" Jessica grunted as she tightened the garrote. Her hands ached from gripping the wooden bar, but she kept applying pressure. Brandis batted at her face, but his weak attempts couldn't hurt her now. He hadn't had any oxygen for over a minute and his carotid arteries were dissecting. Blood leaked from his nose as the vessels tore themselves open. The bearded author began to stroke and asphyxiate at the same time.

He was as good as gone, Jessica just had to wait for his body to realize it was dead.

Finally, Brandis gave up his struggle. His hands dropped away from his neck. His body shuddered then fell onto the floor, where a dark pool of urine bloomed beneath him.

Jessica sagged, drawing deep breaths with her hands on her knees. *Holy shit, what a workout!* Jon had been a relative pushover despite his size. But this Aussie, he'd been determined!

She wiped sweat, spit, and blood off her face and walked out of the condo to retrieve her suitcase from the car. No one watched her. That was good. She'd almost blown the whole damn thing a couple hours ago by not paying attention while she was driving. *My god, the tragedy that had almost become.* A shiver ran through her; she didn't even want to think about it.

The large Samsonite rolled smoothly over sealed asphalt and skipped up the steps and into the condo. Jessica locked herself in and opened the case in the living room, pulling out her casting supplies. It would be close, but she thought she might have just enough to do them both. She grabbed Brandis and rolled him over, bending down to examine his face. She pet his beard as she took in all of his defining features. The man with no face, hers at last, forever.

"Don't worry, love, your secret is safe with me."

Off-World Kick Murder Squad VI

Daniel Arthur Smith

This is the sixth episode of the serialized novel Off-World Kick Murder Squad. Earlier episodes can be read in the previous Canyons issues

AS THE *JENTU* FELL, the twilight horizon slipped from view and—for the second time in as many days—the fast approaching forest filled the windscreen. I'd managed to buckle into the jump seat, but that didn't diminish the sensation of my belly rushing up to my gut.

Thunderous blasts continued beyond the hull, bouncing the ship between a sandwich of concussions. Then the explosions stopped, leaving the bridge eerily quiet in their absence.

Anson cleared his throat, "*Hrrmm*," then softly said, "Well, at least they've stopped firing."

"They see us going down," said Bailer. "They know were dead in the air."

Anson wasn't fazed. "That's not exactly true."

I wasn't as calm. "What do you mean?"

"I mean we're okay," he said.

"The lights are out. The engines are out. We're falling out of the sky." I threw my hands up but right then, the cabin shook so hard I had to grab back down to the sides of my seat so as not to fall over. "From where I sit, I fail to see how we're okay."

"We will be in a minute," said Anson. "It's not an EMP."

"How do you know?" I asked.

He tugged at the yoke. "Because I still have a heavy stick. Let's just ease back…" Anson pulled back on the yoke and the horizon crept back into view. He reached his arm down by his side, and, with a *click*, a scarlet glow washed over the console. "That's better," he said. "Bailer buddy, how are you doing?"

"Fine," said Bailer.

"And you, Cap?"

"Swell," I said, and I was. "Glad you're the one flying the *Jentu*."

"I appreciate the vote of confidence," said Anson, then he gently tilted to the side. The *Jentu* followed, shifting her glide path toward the shadowed contours of the dark valley below. "I can go another klick or two before we have to set her down, but I'm confident we can reboot before that."

"What do we need to do?" I asked.

"You just sit tight, Cap. Bailer's got this. Those concussion blasts they were firing affected the airflow around the *Jentu* and caused the compressors to stall, which triggered a safety feature, disabling the power. We just need to turn those engine compressors back on."

"Put disabling that safety feature high on your list of things that need doing."

"It's kind of important," said Anson. "The way it's supposed to work—"

I cut him off, "Just put disabling that safety feature on your list."

"Yes, Cap. Bailer, grab that red lever. On three, I'll flip the one on my side and you flip yours. One…two…three."

Zwoosheeep! The console went as flashy as a casino table, stabilizing when all of the control indicators and screens were properly engaged.

"All right," said Anson. "Now to get to the river." He gently turned the yoke and the *Jentu* veered to port. "Okay. Switch off all four of the thruster engines, and when I give you the signal, you turn them all on again."

Bailer nodded. "Got it," he said, then flipped the four toggles down. "Ready on your mark."

What I noticed was the black of a mountainside coming in fast before us. "Anson," I said. "You do see we're running out of valley?"

"Just a second more, Cap."

By that point we were skimming the canopy, and the tallest of the trees began to brush against the underside of the delta wings, abruptly jostling the *Jentu* starboard to port and back. I can tell you, the jump seat was becoming mighty restrictive and with each bump I was getting a bit more uneasy.

"Any time would be good."

"Just a sec..."

"You keep saying that, but I don't know that we have a second more."

"And there it is," said Anson. "Hold on."

"There it is what?"

"The waterfall."

"Waterfall?" I asked.

"We're about to go over," said Anson. "Hold on tight. Bailer, get ready."

I wasn't ready. "Over a waterfall? Why do we have to go—"

Then the nose of the *Jentu* took a radical dive down and before my eyes, the shadowy top of the canopy beyond the windscreen disappeared to a wide opening of darkness then—the boiling white waters of the river below.

I white-knuckled the sides of my seat and pulled myself into it. "*Whooooaa*," I yelled as the river rushed closer and my gut raced to my head.

Anson reached to the throttle quadrant of the helm and grabbed 'hold of the master lever. "Now!" he yelled.

Bailer threw all four of the switches up.

Zweeeee-EEEERRRRR! The thrusters ignited and Anson pushed the master lever forward.

RRRRR!

The engines roared loudly and the bridge quaked and shuddered so much, I had to clench my teeth from the rattle; then just like that, Anson pulled the *Jentu* from the dive, up toward the soft purple of the morning sky.

"We'll still have to set down to do diagnostics and repairs," he said.

"And to disable that safety feature," I added. "Nothing too safe about a stall while being pursued by anyone less than happy with us."

"Yes, Captain."

The foul odor that had permeated the bridge began to rapidly dissipate, filtered so quickly through the life support system, you wouldn't think the cabin had been smoke filled a moment before. I clicked off the safety buckle, freed myself of the jump seat, then hit the comm. "Is everyone all right down there?"

Cassidy answered. *"Anything that wasn't secured tight found a new place. Are we going to make a habit of this?"*

"I think not," I said. "I'll be down in a minute." I stepped between Anson and Bailor and placed a hand on their shoulders. "Great job, fellas."

They both responded with a cheery, "Thanks, Cap."

"Let's get a ways away before setting down. Bailer, you help him out."

Bailer said, "Sure thing." And Anson added, "It won't take long."

"Good," I said. "I want to get to sky sooner than later. If you need anything, let me know. I'm going down to help out the others and tend to our guest."

By the time I made it below, Cassidy, Rhia, and Rhoe were already picking up the pillows, clothes, and whatever else hadn't been secured. The only sign left of our near catastrophe was a bit of clutter strewn across the galley. My concern was our new guest and the reason for our mission: Cerulean Blue. So I went past the galley in the passenger dorm. There I found Hodge leaning against the wall outside of a spare cabin. He had his nose buried in a vid card. "Are you watching something from the Archive?" I asked.

"Alice in Wonderland," he said.

"I told you this place ain't like that."

He shrugged. "I know. But I like the story."

I peeked into the passenger cabin. Cerulean was seated on the end of the bunk at the far side of the room, rubbing his long, thin, scaled hands together above the heat vent.

"How's our guest?" I asked.

"Oh. He's fine," said Hodge. "Me? I've got the willies. It's those eyes. Just ain't right. Are you sure we're related to him?"

"Well. They say that the lizard men are the forerunners of the syn technology."

"Does that mean that syns, me and you and every other thing synthetic has a lizard brain?"

"No," I said. There may be more than some truth to that, but I didn't care to confuse Hodge any further. "He's from Indicus, the Blue

Plane, and they're the founders of the technology. That's the only thing in common."

"Still gives me the willies."

I gave Hodge a nod and, without lifting his eyes from vid, he moved away from the door.

"Go help the girls," I said, "I'll want to chat with him for a bit."

"Okay," said Hodge. He couldn't have slipped past me any faster.

I stepped back to the door then, as my augments assessed the reptoid, I hesitated in a thought of my own. Cerulean had a foot on me at least, and at the end of those thin, bluish scaled hands were long, deep blue nails that could easily shred through me without much effort on his part, not to mention those dagger teeth. He could have taken any one of us out at his own choosing, which meant he'd chosen not to. But Hodge was right about those eyes. They were unsettling—or, I should say, those swirls of light where his eyes should be.

Now you might be thinking I'd be used to seeing eyes glow, living with syns and being a syn myself. But that isn't how it is. For the most part, the pupils of our eyes just happen to be a brighter color blue than most mortals, a cerulean blue that, in the right light, glows iridescent in the same way as a cat—if you ever saw a cat that wasn't a syn, I mean. Cats and most vertebrates have a layer just behind the retina called the tapetum lucidum, and it reflects the incoming light and thus increases night vision. Humans don't have that, unless they're Bureau Boys or modded like us.

That blue iridescent layer we have is due to the integration of organic, ocular, and neural tech—that tech being neural lace. The neural lace weaves through the brain, nervous system, and drapes right down behind our retinas, enhancing our vision and producing a glow—just like the layer of tapetum lucidum cats have. And it's the neural lace that links us back to Cerulean and his people.

A bit of history.

Like I said before, Cerulean is Indici, which means he's from the blue Indicus Plane. When the humans stumbled upon the Indici, they discovered that the ancient Indici technology was vastly superior to anything the humans had for themselves. At first, the Indici withheld their tech–hid it really–because they didn't like the humans. But then came the Battle of Uluru and the Spectral Wars, and that's when the Indici, albeit reluctantly, began to share—they hated humans, but they hated the invading Omni forces even more. The Indici were the ones who helped the Alpha Plane advance in crystal technology and, through organic synthetics, feed the homeland.

That's where we come in.

The first syns in the homeland were mechanical constructs. It was the Indici technology that led to organic synthetics. First hybrids, then fully programable organics—steel became bone. Organic synthetics are based on Indici physiology, programmed at creation with basic forms of neural lace. The neural lace is how our basic consciousness–the template for a soldier, a worker, a companion–is uploaded ready-made into our syn shells. That's how we're wide awake on day one, and leveraging that neural lace tech was our fall back plan for Will—if he was still in there.

We aren't the only ones to use it. The humans use neural lace too; they can also transfer consciousness to syn shells and vice versa, like that time Cassidy transferred into that blood broker—but that's another story.

Nobody is quite sure how the Indici use the lace. Some say just to regenerate and that the lizard bodies aren't even their original form. Nobody in the Alpha Plane knows for sure. But my point is, at the end of the day, *we* have eyeballs but the eyes of Cerulean Blue were orbs of blue flame.

Now I could've entered into the conversation sternly. But I decided to show Cerulean some kindness. Reason being, like I said, he could have taken any one of us out and he'd chosen not to.

I rapped my knuckles on the door jamb. "Mind if I join you?"

"Pleassse do," said Cerulean Blue. "I'm enjoying the heat. It wasss ssso caw-old in that sssell."

"I imagine," I said. I took a seat in a chair in the corner across from him. "The *Jentu* tends to run hot. Usually a bit much for me. But it must be real nice for you. After being in that ice-box and all."

"The persssissstance of caw-old causssesss an ache-uh. I'm already feeling ssso much better." His head spasmed again in that weird lizard way and he fixed a stare in my direction. "Thank you," he said. "For liberating me from thossse confinesss."

"It was my pleasure," I said.

"You and your caw-rew. You are sss'ynthetics. Are you…" He paused, but I understood what he was asking.

I raised a brow. "Are we humans in syn skins? No. We're pure syn."

The reptoid softly chuckled, "*Ka, ka, ka, ka.*" At least that's what I think he was doing. It put an easy smile on my face. "What isss your name, sss'yn?"

"Eller," I said. "At your service."

"Pleasssure to meet you, Ellahr."

"Likewise. Except I don't know your name."

"And yet you sssaved me."

"Well. The people who hired me gave me a code. They called you Cerulean Blue."

"How fasss'cinating. You may call me Sss'karo."

"Sss'karo," I said with a nod. "So, Sss'karo. Those people in the compound had you in a cell. I'm not going to lie, I'm not partial to any of the five syndicates, or humans in general. So it's my bet they just weren't being all that hospitable. Am I correct about that?"

"You are caw-rrect."

"I'd also like to think it's a safe bet that you're peaceful and I'm not going to have to keep you confined to this room?"

"You are again caw-orrect."

"All right then. You're free to move around our little ship. There's protein in the galley you can help yourself to. No one will give you issue, but I should let you know, it's not every day we have a guest from the Blue Plane. In fact, this is the first time any of us onboard have actually met an Indici."

"I undersss'tand. I will kaw-cep my profile low."

"That is much appreciated."

"You sss'erve me an honor with your trust."

"It will make it much easier if we all get along." I stood up. "I'm sure you noticed the engine stall?"

"I did."

"It's remedied, but we'll have to briefly set down to go over the ship, then we'll be on our way and off world before you know it."

I kept my face to him as I stepped back through the doorway— keeping as casual and calm as I could make it look. I was about to turn and leave when he stopped me.

"Captain Ell-ah," he said. "You mentioned that you were hired?"

I had and that was admittedly a slip on my part. I would've preferred to make the rendezvous to deliver Sss'karo without furthering that point of discussion.

"Yes," I said. "I did mention that. That we were hired, I mean. I told you I wasn't going to lie, and I won't. It's like this. We do jobs. We don't ask questions. Now, some people were concerned about your situation and asked us to spring you. So we did." I started to turn again, thinking to slip away before Sss'karo asked another question. But he did anyway.

"And I'm free to go?"

"We were asked to save you, then deliver you to their safety. So that's what we're doing."

"Do you trussst them?"

And there it was. "Like I said. We do jobs. We don't ask questions."

His slender tongue slithered. "Are you curiousss asss to why I was being held?"

"I am not," I said. Of course I was. But start asking too many questions and you'll hit upon some you might not like the answers to.

"I wasss betrayed, held against my will."

"Well, I figured that, judging by the steel bands that bound you to that chair."

"I am much older than I appear. I sssplit with my people of the plane that share your planet eons ago, and have sssince inhabited the Indicusss Plane of this world. I believe that the Sss'yndicate wantsss technology and that they abducted me eith-aw to gain insightsss into my counterpartsss, or they are operating under the auspicesss of thossse sss'ame allied Indici."

"I appreciate you sharing, and though either of those things may be, in part or in total, true, it's no concern of mine."

"Do the people you are taking me to really wish for my freedom or do they want what they think I possess for themssselves?"

"Again, not a concern of mine."

"It should be."

"And why is that?"

"Because what I know could mean your end."

With those parting words, I went back to the bridge.

Not everything that Sss'karo said was clear to me, other than him believing that what he knew was something dangerous. But just what that danger was, or whether he meant it would be a harm to all life in general or particularly syns, wasn't clear to me. I didn't take it as a threat. If he wanted us dead, we would be. My bet was that he was looking to sway me to his favor and away from the mission at hand. Yet even knowing that, I couldn't shake the feeling his words had left me with. I usually wouldn't let anything get under my skin, but there was something about Sss'karo, and it didn't take long for what he said to gnaw into me.

That is exactly why we don't ask questions.

No one ever says anything you truly want to hear. They start speaking and before long, something said burrows into your head and starts you to second guessing yourself.

Anyway, we spent the next few hours heading back the way we came, skimming the canopy to stay stealthy, and when we were satisfied we were far enough away, I told Anson to set her down. He found a forest glade nestled between a high ridge and a small lake, which was a bit of a bonus because it allowed us to cycle water while we were there.

First things first, we did an outside inspection while Anson and Bailer went through every system on the ship. There were a few things to tune up, but nothing that needed repair. The outside was fine too. There was some light scoring from the anti-air fire, but whatever they blew up alongside the ship left no mark.

When Hodge and I were done inspecting, we flushed the purifiers and refilled the water system and reserve tanks. He was heading back toward the shore to pull the hose when he set his sights on a blue plumed, two-legged lizard bird near the water's edge—easily a meter taller than a man.

"You know," he said to me, "that there lizard bird looks like a big old chicken."

"I suppose it does," I said.

"I like chicken. There's that place on Riley where they grill chicken over an open fire. It's synthetic, of course, but it sure does taste good."

"Yeah. I remember that place. That meat was delicious."

Hodge shifted his lower jaw side-to-side as if there was already something in his mouth. "You know," he said, "the way I figure, if he looks like chicken, he should taste like chicken."

"There's only one way to find out," I said. I took a step forward, drew my blaster, and let loose a shot at the lizard's crested head. *Pew.* The tall bird collapsed on the shore.

"Well, all right!" Hodge said as he headed over to the bird.

Cassidy watched from the open loading bay. "Wow," she said. "Fresh water and fresh food."

"I think everyone will be happy with a change in protein."

"Ya," she said. "Sounds great. You know how to cook that thing?"

"I figure Hodge is right," I said. "It's just a big chicken."

"Sure," she said. "Shame we don't have a big oven."

The two of us watched Hodge as he tugged and pulled on the legs of the beast, barely moving it from where it had dropped.

"Hmm," I said. "Looks like we're going to have to cut it up. Aren't we?"

"Looks like," said Cassidy. "I'll get a torch."

There was some effort involved, but we butchered up one of those legs for a roast and froze the rest in the food store. Rhia and Rhoe, being vegetarians, gathered their own treasure of some fresh leeks and plant edibles they found outside the ship and we settled down for a feast. We invited Sss'karo to join us, but he didn't, which was just as well. I wasn't sure what he'd think about the main course. It also freed me up to have an after dinner talk with the squad.

"All right," I said after the last of the food was cleared, "now that we've got our bellies full, I wanted to talk a bit about our next steps."

Hodge raised his glass. "Hear, hear," he said. "Let's get off this rock."

"That's the immediate plan," I said. "It was a little hairy this morning, but we accomplished what we set out to do and as a bonus, we took on fresh water, vegetables, and protein. We've also gone through the *Jentu* and she's good to go. So as soon as the sun sets, we'll head off world to the rendezvous and exchange Sss'karo and the device for the remainder of our fee."

"And where's that?" asked Hodge. "Are you planning on tapping that quant again?"

"No. No quant," I said.

"'Cuz I don't like that," he added.

"First off, it's not a quant, second, our rendezvous is a hop-skimp-jump over to the fourth planet—Mars."

"We're going to Mars?" asked Hodge.

"Yep. Anson charted a flight plan and we'll be there just short of two weeks."

"Two weeks?" said Bailer.

"I think two weeks is fine," said Hodge. "As long as we aren't using that quant device."

"Yeah," said Bailer. "I'm with Hodge. But why so long? The solar sail should take half that time."

"I don't want to draw too much attention, being so close to Earth and all."

"Ah, agreed. So if everything is ready, why wait until dark? Albeit, there's less chance of being sighted. But even if we were, we haven't detected anything that could catch us. Unless of course they have some cannons sprinkled across the planet."

"I'd rather slide out peaceful like," I said. "Especially with our cargo."

"Cargo?" asked Hodge. "What's so special about the Indici?"

"He doesn't mean the Indici," said Cassidy. "Do you, Cap?"

"You're right. I don't. Downing this land bird gave me an idea. Anson looked it up. Tell them what you found."

Anson lifted a digital pad from beside him, tapped it, and projected a 3D holo-image that resembled the lizard bird. "According to the Archive, what we found is an *ornithomimid* which, for those of you who have tried it, is a particularly tasty creature. Now, it's supposed to be extinct, and there ain't nothing exactly like it being farmed anywhere."

Cassidy chimed in. "So you want to haul a load of the birds to Mars."

"Exactly," I said. "Most of the new Mars settlements are agricultural, fresh in the new terraformed atmosphere. A creature like the ortho...orno—"

Anson corrected, "Ornithomimid."

"Ornithomimid," I repeated. "A creature like this would be welcome. I say it's a safe bet that if we load up the hold with as many of these as we can carry, we'll be able to turn them for a tidy profit."

"Right," said Bailer. "I get it, and we could use the credits. But how are we supposed to explain how it is that we came upon these dinosaurs?"

"We just tell the farmers that they're synthetic," said Hodge. "Just like the little chickens on Riley."

Everyone looked at Hodge.

"What?" he said.

"That's a great idea," said Cassidy.

"Well, yeah," said Hodge. "That's why I said it. For an extinct bird, it is delicious. I mean, the dinner was excellent. So much better than eating protein paste, and I'm sure the Martian folk will feel the same way."

I shot Hodge a wink. "That's what I was thinking."

"Too bad there was only one of them," he said. "And we ate it."

"Oh," said Cassidy. "There are plenty more out there. I was just outside gathering the laundry and there was a group grazing by the edge of the lake."

"You don't say," I said. "Let's go take a look."

And just like Cassidy said, there was a whole herd, or flock, of those lizard birds gathered together in threes and fours of like colors—scarlet reds, brilliant indigo blues, and some crested in gold.

"Let's go round them up," I said.

"Round them up?" asked Cassidy.

"Steer them into the ship. It will be easy."

Which is exactly what we did.

And it was surprisingly easy. We staked some line in a vee away from the loading bay then I went with Hodge, Bailer, and Cassidy to flank them and together, we walked them toward the ship. Not so fast as to upset them–they were easily agitated–just enough to keep them moving.

Once they were inside, we closed the lift gate, then gathered up some of the lake moss and grasses we'd seen them feeding on.

We'd finished loading the bay ahead of schedule with daylight to spare, so we decided to take of advantage and go. We were moments from leaving when Anson called me over the ship's comm. "Cap," he said, "you might want to take a look at this."

I went up to the bridge with Hodge by my side. Anson and Bailer were leaning over the console veering out into the clearing beyond the ship.

"What is it?" I asked. "What are you looking at?"

Bailer stepped aside to give me space. "Something's upset the lizards."

I leaned forward to see for myself. "I'll be," I said. Lizards as small as your hand were skittering on two legs over the ridge through the clearing right alongside more of those lizard birds, and more than a few other four-legged varieties every other size in between.

"They're spooked," said Hodge. "You think it's that big fella we ran into last night?"

"I don't know," I said. "Could be. Something's certainly stirred them up. Are we good to go?"

"That we are, Cap," said Anson.

"Then let's get to doing just that."

Anson resumed his startup routine, throwing switches, checking this and that. The lights and screens of the console came back to life. I turned to go back below.

"Cap," he said.

"What's that?"

"We might have a problem."

He tapped the radar scope. The small console screen was lit up with a wave of color-coded dots moving in our direction from just beyond the ridge.

"That's not good," I said.

"Aren't those just more lizards?" asked Hodge.

"Not in formation. Anson, let's go."

The red emergency light went to blinking and the *Jentu*'s klaxon sounded.

"We're marked," said Anson.

"Shut that thing off," I said, then leaned forward again to the windscreen. A field of red squares filled my augments, scattered across the column of troopers and half a dozen artillery mechs topping the ridge.

We weren't going anywhere.

34

Tales from the Canyons of the Damned in Space 6

NATHAN M. BEAUCHAMP

CHARLES BAROUCH

TERRY R. HILL

THEY'RE BACK!!!

PRESENTED BY USA TODAY BESTSELLING AUTHOR

DANIEL ARTHUR SMITH

Exclusionary Symbiosis
Nathan M. Beauchamp

DASHER'S RADIAL ENERGY MATRIX roasted well over a thousand bugs a second, and that suited Jaxson just fine. He'd grown to like the sizzle of the bugs frying. It was just about the only thing he took any joy in since arriving at Delta Centauri. Cruising at ninety knots, the matrix burned an estimated 67,000 bugs a minute, almost four million an hour. A rain of guts that reminded him of his grandma's lemon meringue pie filling fell over the still living bugs churned beneath *Dasher's* wake.

A glaze of orange light shrouded *Dasher's* cockpit, giving the endless oncoming swarm of insects a distinctive amber glow. Jaxson spat a stream of tobacco against the inside of the matrix—the real stuff, not the fake shit hawked at Kniles Exploratory. It slid down the interior wall and dribbled onto stained decking. Twenty-thousand volts on the outside, safe as kittens on the inside. Another bit of wizardry cooked up by the eggheads back at Earth. He sometimes wondered how they'd they tested the energy matrix. Go-fast boats racing across a Louisiana Bayou, shredding dragon flies and thumb-sized mosquitos? Because despite the fancy name, the matrix wasn't much more than a super pricey bug zapper.

And there were a shit ton of bugs to zap on Delta. Nothing but bugs, other than the three-story tall, fibrous plants reminiscent of broccoli. The bugs ate the plants in the warm months, popped out trillions of new young, died, and fertilized the decimated plants for the next growing season. The scientists called it "the most extreme form of exclusionary symbiosis ever discovered." Bugs. Plants. Life. Death. The scientists figured it had all been going on for over a hundred million years, other forms of life on Delta expunged.

It pissed Jaxson off that the first life aside from bacteria that humans had discovered on one of the half-dozen Earth-like planets reached by humans was nothing more than worthless bugs. He'd only signed up for Delta when he'd heard there'd be bugs to kill. He'd grown up watching the same old classic movies as other grunts: the fifteen-part *Starship Troopers* series; *Aliens*—the original movies and the remakes; the new-wave B-movies like *Sector Nineteen*. Fighting bugs seemed like the right mix of glamor and danger something to tell girls about on furlough. He'd never imagined it would be about as exciting as driving an old taxi through a bug hurricane.

The bugs had no end, and despite the muted savage pleasure he took in exterminating them, he could run supplies from the landing site at Kniles out to Proxima research station for two lifetimes and not make a dent in the alien population. *Aliens*. What a joke that had turned out to be.

They'd given up on trying to send orbitals directly to Proxima. Constantly shifting magnetic fields played chaos with nav systems, and extreme winds made landings hazardous. After a second orbital ended up nose-first in Delta's loamy soil, the higherups made the call to run skiffs like *Dasher* from Kniles to Proxima and back. It might have been an interesting job if it required actual piloting. But no—*Dasher* followed beacons a meter deep in the ground, the AI-assist running the course without any intervention on Jaxson's part. He was along for the ride as a maintenance tech, and usually spent the three-hour journey watching vids on his handscreen, eating, or staring out into the whirl of bugs, wishing he was on a torch ship back to Earth.

Nav control let out an all-too-cheerful chime. Another beacon crossed. Twenty minutes to Proxima. Jaxson stood and stretched his back. He hoped they'd be serving the spaghetti dinner at Proxima mess. The scientists had good food, he'd give them that. What the hell they were researching at Proxima? Well that was a big goddamned secret, way above his paygrade. Not that he didn't get curious. The same bugs and plants stretched from one end to the other of Delta's single continent. What was different at Proxima?

Another chime. Another beacon crossed. One hundred and eighty in total, he counted them subconsciously on each journey. Only nineteen more to go.

Another chime.

Then a sound Jaxson had never heard before. A sizzling *pop*, almost like a coil gun bolt lancing out to strike a target. But the sound came from *inside* the skiff. Another sizzling pop, and the matrix fell away, exposing the hull to a crush of insects. Jaxson leapt to his feet. Then his feet left the deck and he was suspended for a half-second, just long enough to know that what came next was going to hurt like hell.

The deck slammed into his chest and he bounced.

The skiff tilted sideways.

Jaxson managed a bloody mouthed, "Shit," before the front windbreak caved and bugs roiled through the bent opening. He had the presence of mind to grab a wall stantion before the skiff hit ground for the final time. His arm damn near ripped free of his shoulder when it did.

Shaking with adrenaline, his skiff grounded, Jaxson took a few painful breaths of the remaining oxygen before the rest vented out into Delta's hydrogen-helium air. He forced his battered body toward the emergency locker.

Bugs crawled over the outside of the locker.

Pink, pearlescent, winged, thumb sized—something like a wasp but without stingers. Three body sections like an insect, eight legs like an arachnid. Jaxson was too shook up to care about the bugs picking their way up his uniform pants or the bugs exploring the blood oozing out of a deep gash in his dislocated left arm. *Training. Follow your training.* He got out the mask, breathing apparatus, exo assist module. *Mask first, activate the chest pack, three controlled breaths...* Cool air laced with pain killers filled his lungs. *Activate neuro controls to link to the exo...*

Serpentine bands found his ankles, quads, waist, and the exo blossomed around his body, supporting his weight with biopneumatics and synthetic muscle fiber. The meds had enough kick to make the rollout process both surreal and euphoric. He was like a bug himself now, body shrouded and strengthened by the exosuit. Maybe it was just the drugs, but for the first time in months, Jaxson felt a small burst of happiness.

Emergency procedures complete, Jaxson looked around the skiff, trying to locate the source of the critical failure. A bit of oily smoke lingered in the cabin and streaks of electrical burn marred the nearest control board. Massive electrical blowout, maybe from the capacitors that kept the matrix humming. Once the matrix dropped, insects had filled the jets and destroyed them. Far more than he could fix. He hoped the AI-assist had notified Kniles of the crash before losing power. If it had, all he needed to do was wait for help to arrive.

Thousands—tens of thousands—of bugs had made it inside the cabin. They clung to every surface, crawled over the exosuit, fluttered against his face mask. How he'd managed to get that on without trapping bugs inside he'd never understand, but he was damned grateful that at least his face was free of bugs.

The dull thrum of distant pain played in harmony with his elevated heartrate. Seconds became minutes. No com, no sat link, and magnetic fields too strong to pierce with his in-suit radio. What if the colossal failure had wiped the AI-assist before it could message Kniles? What if nobody knew what had happened? They'd figure it out, eventually, when *Dasher* didn't make her arrival time at Proxima. But how long would that take? Longer than his oxygen supply?

Be calm. You've got ten hours' worth. Help is on the way.

But what if it wasn't?

He checked the supply gauge on his oxygen. The analog dial seemed to be moving faster than it should. He'd already dropped below the eight-hour mark. How was that possible? Was he leaking air?

He checked the supply, the line, the mask. Found no fault.

But the dial was working its way downward, and fast.

The skiff was *filling* with bugs. Bugs up to his ankles. Bugs on top of bugs. What if they stuffed the skiff to the brim? What if so many bugs piled inside he couldn't get back out?

Jaxson didn't make the decision to exit the skiff so much as leaving became an absolute necessity, like when he'd emptied his guts in the middle of mess after coming down with some sort of super bug. *Super bug.* The words rattled inside his hollowed-out skull. Ideas were getting damned blurry. Was that from the meds?

Outside, Delta's blue light gave the bugs a much different appearance, their milky bodies a burnished sapphire as they dove and skittered beneath the harsh shadows cast by the broccoli towers. Jackson had never seen them like this, nothing but a face plate between his eyeballs and them. Their slow and rhythmic movement was so different from the pelting deluge caused by the skiff's speed. They had a stately air to them. Unhurried yet purposeful.

The oxygen dial reached seven and a half hours, though only a minute or two had passed. Jaxson did some quick mental math. He'd need to hurry to reach Proxima before he exhausted his air supply. Assuming the leak wasn't getting worse. If it came down to that, he'd take off the mask and let the local air knock him unconscious. A better way to go than sucking at scraps of oxygen. Maybe the bugs would eat his body. That'd be fair, considering how many of the bastards he'd killed in his short time on Delta.

Delta's home star had started to sink in the southern sky, further lengthening the broccoli tower shadows. Jaxson trudged over loose soil, leaving giant, exosuit boot prints behind. A great accompaniment of bugs seemed to follow at each side, whirling and darting, some taking a brief rest on his exosuited body. He thought of flicking them free, but decided it wasn't worth the effort. The bugs couldn't do him any real harm.

Meters beneath his feet, interconnected hives linked by countless passageways ran. Linked in the same way as the broccoli towers' root systems intertwined, an even larger biomass than Earth's aspen groves. He'd seen images of cross-sections of the hives. The bugs had no queens like earth's ants or bees. Every bug could lay eggs, and every bug could fertilize them.

With night coming on fast, the wind picked up, whipping past his helmeted ears at thirty knots. No way could he make much forward progress without the exosuit. He pushed on into the stream, visor HUD laying down a silver pathway over the soil. It took him eight minutes to reach the next beacon, and by that time, his oxygen supply was down to six hours.

He wouldn't make it to Proxima before he ran out.

Like hell I won't.

Through the neuro connect, he boosted power to the exo muscle fibers and began to run, taking giant leaps forward in Delta's seventy-three percent of Earth's gravity. Each leap rattled his ribcage and sent shudders of pain down his spine, pain too strong for the meds to dull. He might beat his body to a pulp in the process, but he was going to make it to *Proxima.*

On his next forward leap, the rubberized foot pads of the exo slammed through Delta's crust, miring him up to his shins in soil.

Momentum carried him forward headfirst, sprawled out, wind knocked from his chest. It took many painful seconds to regain his air. He pushed upright, trying to breathe steadily, trying to save as much oxygen as he could—

A bug hovered directly in front of his faceplate. He blinked, thinking the fall had somehow affected his vision. Blinked again. The bug remained, wings rotating like copter blades, its eyeless face inline with his own. Twenty times larger than it should be, its bulbous abdomen tipped by a distinctive, silver-blue stinger.

Jaxson lashed out at the bug with a closed fist.

Too late.

The stinger tip punctured the exo like a knifepoint through cellophane. Agony. Blinding, maddening agony, too intense to allow a scream, every muscle taught as though hit with a stun baton. Agony that faded, dulled, became a warm current flowing through his veins. He slumped to his knees, the giant bug's hooked feet clinging to the exosuit. The pain dissipated, replaced by profound calm. He let himself fall onto his back, still face-to-eyeless face with the bug. In a half-second, he relived the dozens of journeys he'd made from Kniles to Proxima, the tens-of-billions of bugs he'd destroyed. He regretted that so much. So, so much. He saw how wrong he had been, how wrong fleet command had been for coming to *Delta* in the first place.

Not Delta. No, this place had another name. A much more ancient name that could only be spoken with a series of sub-audible clicks and the whirl of wings...

You will help us.

He almost laughed with joy.

He *would* help. He would undo what had been done.

Dimly, as if from the vantage point of another set of eyes, he saw the oxygen meter pass its halfway point. It didn't concern him. Didn't concern *us.*

Us. This time the laugh broke free, gurgling upward out of his swollen stomach. Bloody saliva streaked his lips and chin. *Us.* Filled to overflowing with so many, many, many. A gift for the hot bodies at Proxima. He saw—not with eyes but with the shadowy shapes produced by sound waves—the shuffling, pasty, malformed bodies of the scientist descending cold vertical shafts into the under-deep. Down to where the third participant in the symbiosis of life and death, of eating and reproducing, dwelled in secret darkness. Disturbed, removed, and cut open. Hurt and more hurt caused by the hot bodies, each protected by sunhot burn walls that not even the strongest of them could penetrate.

Rage burned within.

Rage, and a need to set things right.

Us.

How could rage and joy be so intimately intertwined?

Buoyed by a thousand-thousand kin, they flew through the mounting dark, onward to *Proxima.*

Ship of the Dead
Charles Barouch

PLANET-BOUND FOLK DON'T understand what it's like to mine asteroids. We don't get to take anything for granted, like air, water, or even a place to die. Eighty percent women up here. Seventy percent black. That makes The Belt one of the few places where I'm in the majority. I don't do the mining myself. That's another thing the grounders don't think about: for the mines to work, someone has to be up here to patch up ships, cook food, and do other necessary things. Me, I haul bodies to where the sun can pull them in and burn them proper. Just one of the curve balls life threw me.

Yesterday was a hard one. Mine on *2008 AZ* collapsed. Lost my best friend and a lot of drinking buddies. Worse is, I had to mourn them and haul them. Hard to pretend all that "in a better place" crap when you watch them flame out.

"Brenna!" Harley screamed through the comm.

"I hear you same, shout or not," I said. "What fresh hell you got for me, Harley Baer?"

"We have a complaint," he said.

A complaint. Now that was a new one on me. My fares don't have anything left to say by the time I get them. I waited instead of answering, mostly 'cause I knew it would annoy him. That man thought he was my boss. He should remember that I pay him, not the other way around.

"Some damn per-son-age of the grounders thinks you did something wrong," Harley said.

I asked him for details and got a lot of nothing for my troubles. That meant I couldn't handle it from the deck of the *Yawn* like I wanted to. I'd have to come back to base and check the logs. I don't know why I keep him. He's lazy. He don't ask good questions. He don't keep good notes. I have to push him to do each little thing. 'Course, that's why he has the time to work for me. Everyone had already shut the door on old Harley Baer.

I set the autopilot for base and went in for a nap. I figured I could get in three or four hours given the normal jam at the dock. Turned out to be closer to five.

"*Yawn*, you are clear for Northside Slips, proceed to berth four," said the Traffic Control Warden.

It was archaic and stupid. The ship took the instructions and did everything itself. They didn't need to go announcing it. Still, the call was my wake-up signal. Ten minutes to make myself presentable. I showered recent enough, so I used the time to fix an energy drink, sort my hair, and check my credit balance. If I was on base, I might as well resupply and hit a few relaxations.

I stepped off once we were clear. Northside had good seams, so I didn't need a suit to leave the ship. Southside had that accident back a year or so...lost six folks. I keep track of that sort of stuff; of how many died. Occupational habit. Worst luck for others is my good luck. I hate this job.

My office was just two corridors in from Northside. The warden put me in near a berth, so it was a quick walk. Harley, to my shock, was actually doing his job when I walked in. He had a customer sitting with him and he'd even remembered to beam her a rate sheet. I saw my logo on the flimsy in her hand. Miracles do happen.

"Harley," I said in my least irritated voice, "when you're done helping that nice lady, how about you and I talk about that call from Earth."

My tone didn't fool him any. He knew I only came back early 'cause he was being an ijit. The lady looked up and I realizes she wasn't one of us. This was a grounder, up here in my crappy little office. She wasn't a new client. She was the problem I came to figure out.

"I'm Allison Washington," she said. "You must be Brenna Childs."

"I must," I said, attempting a joke.

It didn't land. She looked at me like I was stupid. I started to reach for my hair—a nervous habit—but I stopped myself from giving in to the urge. She just kept staring. It was like some sort of a contest. I broke first.

"What can I do for you?" I finally said.

"I'm from Beyonder Services. We run the part of the government which licenses your business," Ms. Washington said.

She showed me her flimsy, which now displayed her credentials instead of my rate sheet. I pulled mine out of my pocket and unrolled it. She made a flicking gesture and her details beamed over. I made a point of looking, 'cause you should. I didn't care what it said. People like me end up dancing for people like her all the time. The particulars didn't matter. Not this time, not ever.

"So, what'd I do wrong? Not common for ground...er, planet-bound folk to visit," I said.

"Oh, no, nothing like that," Ms. Washington said. "We are here to see about expanding your charter."

"My business only gets bigger if people die," I said. "Are you in the business of killing folks?"

"I'm explaining myself badly," Ms. Washington said. "We expect that emigration from Earth to the Beyond will be rising. Since there are only two of you in your...unique line of business..."

"Let me guess," I said. "You mean me and Pegger Smith. And you can't seem to get Pegger's attention? And now I have to explain to you what I've already told twenty others just like you. Pegger was in the business. She had a nice little ship called the *Dawn Fire*. When she started getting on in years, she took me on. I was between mines, 'cause the one I was working had played out. We were partners for five years before old Pegger ended up riding in the back, if you take my meaning. I always called the *Dawn Fire* the *Yawn Fryer* because it bugged her. When she died, I made the name official."

"We'll have to update our records," Ms. Washington said.

"That's what the last twenty said," I told her.

She tried to start talking again, so I faked a yawn and asked nicely if we could do this after I'd had a chance to catch up my paperwork and my rest. She bought it and we agreed to meet for dinner.

Southside Inner had a nice Italian place. Never been on Earth, so I can't speak to how authentic it is, but I like it. Odds are, Washington's paying, so I expect to like it extra this time.

105

As soon as the door closed behind her, I lit into Harley. He'd called it a complaint when it wasn't. He didn't tell me it was 'in person' instead of just a 'net thing. He sure as hell didn't tell me she was from Earth when I walked in. And she was government on top of that. If I wasn't the only ijit who could meet her need, that coulda been important.

"Brenna," Harley said when I finally had to pause for breath.

"Yes?" I asked.

"Nothing. You are every ways right," he said.

I knew this act. He sounded contrite. He put up the puppy dog eyes. It always worked on Pegger. Difference was, I wasn't his cousin. She had to put up with him. I ran the list of people who might replace him through my head. Four of them were in yesterday's haul. It looked like I had to put up with him, too. Thing is, none of those four would have taken the job. They liked the life. Me, I was happy to get halfway out. Doing this meant I kept out of the mines but stayed in The Belt. It was a fair deal. Still hate it, though.

"One more screw up, Harley Baer," I threatened, "and we'll see if a live one burns any slower than the dead."

I'd just had my nap, so I used the whole of the stall time to catch up on paperwork. Don't know why we still call it that. I haven't seen anything but a flimsy for three years now. Last I was at the Doc, and she had a diploma. I thought it was paper but she said something about being animal skin. I don't see much of that here either, 'less you count human animals.

Fifteen death certs were waiting on my finish up. Harley could do every part but seal them, but somehow everything was left for me. If I didn't have a legal requirement on having this office, I'd boot his butt back to Earth with one swift kick. That man hit every nerve by the end of any given month.

I did the certs, I paid the bills—also his job—and finished up by ordering some MRE for the Yawn. I get lazy about cooking by the end of a tour and skipping meals can be fatal. Keeping alive takes energy.

My momma used to tell me and my sister Crystal that sharp was the word you needed most in space. Avoid sharp objects. Look sharp. Dress sharp. Keep a sharp tongue so you don't get taken. She used to joke that my sister was named Crystal to remind her to be sharp. Me? I never needed a reminder.

I was prompt to the restaurant, but the government lady wasn't. When you know how much air costs, you resent anyone who makes you waste it. Sitting here, cooling my heels, was just that: waste. When she showed up, she was, as my momma used to say, space blue. It's how grounders sometimes get when they breathe our air for too long. She wasn't acclimating well. For some reason, that made me happy.

I could have gotten up and helped her to the table. I could have told her that every restaurant and store was equipped with gentle-breathers. Instead, I sat and watched her space blues take her lungs for a ride. Whatever we ordered tonight, odds are, I was the only one eating.

"So, you want to up the death rate," I said conversationally.

Washington fumbled a pill case out of her pocket and washed it down with a sip of water. It seemed to work near instant, but that might just be the anticipation lending her strength. When the pill and that sip hit her stomach, I saw it on her face. She kept it together and finally got to talking.

"Burse Co. is expanding and that means less space for people. We in the government have been suing them to give back some of the land, but they are just too big to oppose. We expect perhaps ten percent of the remaining Earth population will be looking at The Belt for living space."

"Ten percent? What's that leave?" I asked. "Sounds to me like you have just enough land to hold the Burse employees and the government ones."

"Closer to the truth than most people will admit," she said.

I'd rather not have been right.

"Fact is, in ten years, there'll be more people in the Beyond than on Earth," she added.

Her conversation was too frank. Things must be worse than I thought if she was admitting this much. 'Course, The Belt can't support that many. Even if most of them go to the Moon and Mars, we're damn close to limits as-is. I didn't say that, though. I wasn't here to school this grounder. I was here to eat some free Italian food and let her talk.

"What do you want me to do?" I asked.

"We want you to spin up two more ships," she said.

I nearly spit out the sip of water I just took. The waitress came by, finally, and I waved her off. I had to hear this proper. How was I going to spin up anything? No money and no crew. Keeping Harley was a luxury. What did she think I made in a month of doing this?

"We'll pay for everything," Ms. Washington said, guessing my train of thought.

That pill must have tilted her brains. Government never gave me anything. They're in the business of taking.

"When you say pay, and I mean this kindly, do you know what spinning up a ship costs?" I asked it as calmly as I could.

"Three million credits for each ship," she said like she was discussing the price of the side dishes, "A quarter more for the refit to meet government regulations. Eight thousand credits to train each captain in final protocols...Do I need to go on?"

"And you're just gonna Fargo me six and a half mil?" I tried to match her casual tone.

"Nine million, even," Ms. Washington said. "Your current ship deserves an overhaul. We might go a little higher if you put in a grant request for a better office."

The waitress came back. I wanted to wave her off, but I didn't have the spare attention to do that. Ms. Washington ordered the fire-roast vegetable appetizer. I guess that pill really did fix her space blues. I was having my own sort of blues. I only owned the *Yawn* because Pegger willed it to me. I'd never earn the three million to buy a stock ship, much less the other costs. Hell, my ship was sixteen years old when I got it, and I couldn't have bought it used, even if you stacked my income for the last five years against it. Damn.

"I'll have papers for you tomorrow," Ms. Washington said as she picked up her water glass.

I just looked at her. She said numbers that big like they bored her. I pointed at something on the menu as the waitress tapped her foot. My mouth still wasn't working. I grabbed up my water because drinking it gave me something to do while I gathered my wits. Be sharp, momma said.

"I'll look over the papers," I said.

When the appetizer arrived, Ms. Washington told the waitress to bill the meal to her account. She finished off one bite of carrot and left. I sat alone. I ate the vegetables while I waited for whatever I'd ordered. When the waitress returned, I was happy to see a steak. Guess that was what I pointed at. 'Case you don't know, free steak tastes extra good. I ordered another. After that, I ordered dessert to go.

I took my bag of zeppole and went back to the ship. I don't maintain apartments on base. That's a cost I don't need to pay. Sleep was hard that night. I had two helpings of steak in my belly and nine million credits dancing in my head. The morning started with a shower and a careful pass through my closet. I needed to look extra sharp.

Ms. Washington was there half an hour after I opened. She beamed me the contracts. I started reading.

"Now, did you think you could slip this past me because I'm home-schooled? Or do you just think that all Beyonders are gullible?" I asked it with venom in my voice.

"We don't slip anything past anyone," Ms. Washington said. "We're the government."

I nearly choked on that.

"Last night, you didn't say anything about this being a loan," I accused. "I can't pay back nine million. Even without interest. And you have that set to ten percent. I thought ten percent interest was illegal."

"Skip to the second document. You can finish the first one later," she said.

I skipped. The second document assigned the debt to Burse Co. To my shock, that one was already counter-signed. Burse was picking up the tab.

"How'd you get them to do it?" I asked.

"Part of how they've been stalling our lawsuit," Ms. Washington said. "They keep donating money to soften the impact of their actions."

"So, I borrow from the government, and Burse gets the payment book?" I asked.

"Take your time reading," Ms. Washington said.

I took my time. There were six contracts in all. They all referenced each other. I was jumping from page to page and document to document. It took me a long time to be sure I didn't miss anything. I found three paragraphs which I'd overlooked on the first pass. I read every bit. Then I read it again. It was a sadistic piece of work. Everything had a rule-set explaining how I was allowed to spend it. Every rule-set had a penalty condition. It'd be like blind-driving in a minefield to get everything done.

Together, the contracts made my head spin but I'm pretty smart so I got through it. When I was done, there were two things which were very clear. No regular person could ever-ever-ever get away the crap in

109

this set of contracts. The other thing was that I had to say yes. With this much free money, they'd get someone to say yes if I didn't.

I sighed and I signed. Ms. Washington gave me a reassuring smile. I didn't feel right about any of this. I remembered my manners and walked her to the docks. The happier she looked, the more my stomach twisted.

Because it was the government, everything took time. From the day I signed, the life I was satisfied with before the contracts, now it felt like a cheap imitation. I was living in the between; still poor but no longer handling it. It made me less sharp. I nearly final-banged the ship twice that first week. Miners mean asteroids. Asteroids mean *pay attention when you fly*.

Eventually, I settled back into my old ways. I wasn't raised to spend money that hadn't arrived. Mama's wisdom was still protecting me. When the transfer finally went through, I was slow to proceed. How do you make peace with spending that much money?

Ms. Washington, who had been unreachable for the last six months, started calling me. She wanted progress reports. I'd agreed to that, so I had to make some progress to report. Harley turned out to be pretty good at evaluating mechanics. I guess everyone has something they can do. We found a decent ship—made by Burse, no surprise—and a local shop to do the refits. Bigger shops on the Moon and Mars, but I like spending local.

The plan was pretty simple. Build one new ship. I'd captain it while *Yawn* got fixed up. Then, at the tail end, buy the other. Finding captains, that was another matter.

It wasn't the long alone times. Most people up here were okay with that. Trouble was, the ones who could navigate—you can't just trust the automatics—already had work. I didn't just want to out-pay their current jobs. I wanted ships to pay for themselves—for the day-to-day costs at least. I even gave Harley a tryout. He final-banged eight times on the simulator, so I didn't let him near the real controls. Deadlines where looming. I needed a break.

Worst luck for others is my good luck. Three mines tapped out at once. That took me from no applicants to plenty. I snatched up the best two, an ore hauler named Smitty and a miner named Doves. They still needed training, but I had barely enough time to get everything done.

Last Mosey had been in service for two months. *Yawn Fryer* was out of repairs. I'd have the third ship in the next week or two. Still needed a name for it. Things were coming together.

Harley found a loophole. Seems that a pilot could skip the training if they could beat the tests without. I took them on *Yawn* and trained the hell out of them for ten days. I hated sharing space on my ship, but I did what needed doing. They passed on the first try. I teamed them up on *Last Mosey* until we had the last ship.

The big day finally arrived. Our third ship was ready. I was back on Northside this time 'cause I'd called *Last Mosey* in so Smitty and Doves could celebrate with me. The predicted influx of grounders had started last month and they were accident prone up here. I'd been very busy. We'd all been busy. I hate when business is good.

With the third ship was arriving, I thought it was going to be a good day. It wasn't. We took in a big lunch while we waited for the *Pegger's Dream* to be delivered. We, my captains and me, were in shock when we walked over to Northside berth sixteen to see our third ship.

She didn't have her name on her nose. Instead, it had a Burse logo and a registration number. Not the logo it had when it came from the factory – 'cause this was a stock Burse ship originally—this one said 'Burse Final Solutions.' A man stepped off the ship. He wasn't from the repair team I hired to refit it. This one had on a grounder business suit. I knew enough to tell he was just a messenger. The grounder made that flicking gesture which beamed something to my flimsy. I took it out of my pocket to look.

*

Ms. Childs,

As a result of the unfavorable conclusion of the government's most recent lawsuit against us, your funding arrangement with Burse Co. has been terminated. Your ships will be taken as collateral until you complete all payments. The current bill, with interest, will be sent under separate cover. In consideration of your situation, Burse Co. is willing to offer you employment in our new venture, Burse Final Solutions. Upon reviewing your most recent flight license renewal, we have determined that you do not meet our standards for pilots. Accordingly, we will make an office job available. The details of that offer will also arrive under separate cover.

To further ease your mind, we intend to offer Winny Smith and Jackie Doves positions as well. We do not, unfortunately, have a position for Harley Baer at this time.

We thank you for doing business with us and look forward to working with you in the future.

- Allison Washington, Director of New Business, Burse Co.

Last Visit to the Park
Terry R. Hill

NINETEEN THOUSAND, FOUR HUNDRED and ninety-six days. Give or take a day or two. Maybe a week. At this point, what difference does it make? That's when everything changed, and sure-as-hell not for the better.

His old bones pushed against his thinning muscles as the cold plastic seat of the subway lurched with every bump of the rails. The car was empty; the only sign of life was a reflection in the window across from him, of an old man sitting and eating a bag of cashews. He wore a coral-colored, droopy fisherman's hat and an unbuttoned, sea blue shirt over a purple t-shirt, with blue and white pinstriped shorts. His body bent as if the world had hung on him for generations. He had been young and strong once, but it was hard to believe those days had blown away so quickly like yesterday's afternoon storm.

Setting the bag of nuts down, he looked to the ring on his left hand; smoothed gold by years of wear, and an insignia surrounded by a black field. That symbol meant something once ago. Something special. Something that people died for. In the end, it meant a lifetime of loneliness, the vacuum within growing stronger while he remained surrounded by millions of strangers; waiting for decades for a familiar face was too much to bear any longer. Tonight, he would do what the Universe was too cowardly to commit; tonight, he would let the cold freeze solid what was left of his heart.

The glass window pane was cold as he slowly drew on the inside frost, watching it melt around his finger. It was the morning evidence he was still alive and not some postmortem dream. This morning, he'd watched the day break as the sun rose far beyond the overcast sky. The muted light was the deciding measure. He had struggled with the decision for quite some time, but the cold, grey morning was the final unbearable metaphor. The memory of his first visit to an old-folks home was still uncomfortably vivid. It was foreign. Everyone was so old, sick, and obnoxiously close to death. The place reeked of lineament, bleach, and shit. Yep, that's exactly how his apartment smelled now. How soon it had happened.

For his entire life, he had looked up at the glinting night sky and felt a longing to explore out in the black expanse of space. Wanderlust is for the young and reckless, but for the last half of his life, it had only grown. A yearning. A quickening of the heart. A calling to go to a home somewhere amid the stars, so strong he would have willingly jumped on any alien ship that stopped by Earth with the promise to go someplace else. Somewhere far beyond his current reach...somewhere he would never see. He would live out the rest of his life and die on this little water-covered rock in the backwoods of the galaxy.

In the last few years, the excitement and longing had been replaced with pain and discomfort from just about every part of his body, plus a few not readily identified. Another new pain that wasn't there the day before, and a few which had been there longer than he could remember. Where had all the years gone? A young man who once started a new life in a faraway place was now an old man; not where he wanted to be. Yes, the decades had flown quickly, but paradoxically he was excruciatingly aware of every single day that had passed. Every doggedly slow minute. It is truly amazing how slow time passes when you're waiting for something very important to arrive but it never does.

Perhaps the years stretched out so long because there was no one with whom he could share them. Those who knew him over the years speculated as to why he never married. Shy, low self-esteem, gay, he'd heard all the gossip, none of it true of course and none of it remotely accurate. Gobsmacked. He'd always loved that phrase. Yes, gobsmacked would be a good way to describe their reaction if they ever knew his actual reason for never marrying.

114

Over the years, he had seen ships, rusted, requiring too much maintenance, spewing too much smoke, threatening to fail at any given moment, and decommissioned before they did. Now he understood how the ships must have felt. Gave all they had to the cause, working tirelessly for the reward of their contract with those they loyally served. However, the reality was they toiled away, day after day until they could go no more, then they were dismantled. And that was why he was going to Central Park today. It was his time. There were record low temperatures forecasted for tonight.

It was time to catch the train to Manhattan.

Normally, it was possible to ignore the typical sounds of the park when he sat and closed his eyes to think, but something niggled for attention in the corner of his mind. More and more of the days were spent this way, thinking about the plans for his life…and how things played out. It wasn't unusual for an old man to ruminate over lost days, but his story was different.

"We're civilized! There were measures put in place to keep this from occurring." Nothing like what happened to him had been heard of for a generation or more. But none the less, it did. Statistics, bad luck, or like the locals say, Karma.

Something poked at his attention again. What was it, a different sound other than the background squeaks of children in the distance or the roar of a plane overhead? Ah. Someone was standing nearby. Their presence weighed heavy like a stranger's shadow on a hot summer afternoon. Honestly, he didn't really care if they existed or not, but idle curiosity eventually won out.

Looking up through untamed eyebrows, he saw a young man standing next to him, dressed in an oversized hoodie, worn leather jacket, and a pair of jeans which appeared to have lost a fight with a wild animal. Of course, with fashion being what it was, it was impossible to tell if he was homeless or going out on the town. The young man's face told a story of harsh living and bad decisions. In the sixties, this young man would have been an outcast, a rebel, a bad seed; but today, he's the norm. The world's expectations and rules had flip-flopped during his life here. How civilization could march on with such reversals was beyond him.

"Hey, old man, anyone sitting here?" the young man asked, pointing at the park bench.

"What?" the old man grumbled. The cold January wind whipped around his head, biting his ears and nose as it tried to get inside his collar.

"I *said*, anyone sitting *here*?" said the young man with an accent and irritation.

The old man scanned the park around him, now empty but for him and this boy. Evidently, the rest of the city had enough sense to stay indoors today.

"Hmmph. Well, since the park's so crowded…if that'll let you die happy, be my guest."

The young man gave what sounded like a grunt of respect to a private joke and flopped down hard next to him. A bit too close, really. Maybe the boy wanted to take his money. Maybe he wanted to kill for the thrill. Maybe he was some perv. Either way, soon, it wouldn't matter much.

A strange smell pricked his nose. Between the dulling of age and living in New York City, one can grow to disregard certain smells, particularly the less pleasant. But this was something different, familiar. Like walking into an old building and the scents suddenly throw you back into your grandmother's home as a youngster, bringing back memories you'd forgotten about decades before. This boy, young man, his presence awakened memories of...

"Why are you sitting here?" the stranger asked.

"I do mind, the question. Who taught you conversational etiquette, a bouncer?" He glanced over to the young man without any discernable emotion. The dangerous ones were generally devoid of emotion. But for what he had planned today, anything violent would be a welcome end to it all.

"Fine...nothing."

"You know it's gonna be freezing soon."

"Thank you for minding my business, young man, but I need the fresh air. Now go away," he growled, immediately regretting engaging in another conversation with a stranger.

The young man nodded his head slightly and turned to look at him, the blankness gone and replaced with controlled irritation.

"You live around here?"

Damn, this boy won't catch a hint.

"Long enough to mind my own business. Look, I really don't want any company today. *Particularly* today." He didn't care any longer.

116

Might as well piss the thug off and have him quickly and silently slide a thin blade between two ribs of his choice, take is ring, and move on.

Un-phased, the young man continued, "You have family close by? Where do they live?"

That did it, that was the last straw of nosiness!

"Look, son! I don't know what your game is—rob me, follow me home and steal my stuff later, try and steal my identity. Whatever your scam is, you should know that I have seen and heard it all before, and I am not your average senior citizen. So, keep your questions and your damn curiosity to yourself. Got it? Otherwise, I'm going to introduce you to a nice can of mace and a conversation with the police!" the old man said with a ferocity not matching his weathered exterior. The muscles of his face were in their practiced place of successful staring down both man and beast.

Slowly, the young man leaned in closer, his voice teetering on a decision as he placed a hand inside his jacket.

"Calm. Down."

The muscles in the old man began to relax a little with the inevitability of what this miscreant was about to deliver. He finally crossed the line. It wasn't how he'd planned it, but what was in his life?

"Sorry, just today I have something to do and having company…complicates things," he mumbled, backed down, and went back to picking through his bag of nuts, which was a better use of his time than telling his story to this damn whippersnapper. The young man looked away.

Pregnant moments passed.

The young man suddenly shifted, facing him again.

Why won't he leave?

"Look, old man, I…don't have much time. What's your story?"

Oh, he could tell him a few things to speed this all along. Maybe a second helping of minding his own damn business perhaps. Or some, 'Keep your perversion to yourself,' or perhaps some, 'Most people don't want to be your damn friend, particularly when they're trying to kill themselves!'

But…anything to get him to move on or do him the favor of quickening his plans along.

"Look, son, I'm not trying to be mean. Well okay, maybe I am, but at my age, I'm not going to apologize for that. It's just that no one has ever wanted to hear my story. I lived a life, but half of it no one can relate to, and I have something to do today."

"Proceed, but let's not prolong this," the stranger locked gaze with him, his cold eyes piercing deep inside of him. A shiver ran across his scalp.

"I mean what I said. No one, including you, can relate to most of my life. Let me speak slowly so it will sink into your young, thick head—you won't understand and think I'm crazy. It's a waste of my time," he snapped, returning to his nuts.

Think he was crazy? Maybe the reactions from the few he'd told his story to over the years were more accurate than he'd been willing to accept. Numerically speaking, if the same conclusion is reached multiple times via independent paths, it tends to represent reality. Maybe it's not a problem of the locals not being able to stretch their minds around his story. Maybe it was him who continued to stretch a story around a reality he didn't want to accept; a deluded narrative he continued to tell himself to cover for something missing in his life.

"Captain Radnower, sir," said the young man. A hint of a slight smirk threatened as his intense eyes continued to probe for something lost, then he growled, "Bet you didn't expect that, huh?"

"Captain? Were you with the Air Force or Navy?"

Radnower paused. "Yeah. I've seen my fair share of unbelievable stuff. Besides, who am I? Just an asshole on a park bench, like you. Try me, but let's not drag this out," he moved his hand from inside his jacket to rest on his leg.

A series of honks from a car in the distance passed as he considered the youth's offer. He gave Radnower a doubtful look. His gut told him to move and find some people for safety, but something else kept him on the bench.

What the hell, he'd entertain telling the story one more time. Morbid fascination of a man who had nothing to lose, won the roll of the dice to see how this would pan out. What did it matter now anyway? "Oh, all right, but I'll tell you again, you're wasting both our time."

Radnower nodded to continue, then slowly scanned the old man's jacket and pockets where his hands were buried.

"Fine, damnit. My name is Lieutenant Colonel Adis Nothan of the Lanthian Space Force, Cartography Wing," Adis began in an old man's 'arthritic sweet' time. "I was sent to this sector of the galaxy to survey and update the star maps."

"Lieutenant Colonels don't update maps," snapped Radnower.

"Yes, well, actually you're right, but," Adis paused, taken aback at the oddly germane remark, "I'd retired from a career in the Force, but I missed it so much and didn't really know how to live as a civilian. I re-enlisted with the cartography group so I could do a little traveling."

Radnower smirked and nodded slowly.

"They gave me a beautiful, one-seater recon scout ship - she was a beaut - and we sailed the winds that blew between the stars.

"My attention was drawn to this planet when I started picking up some very faint signals in the radio frequencies which were unusual for a star system like this. So, once I narrowed it to this unexpectedly habitable blue planet, I went into a circularized orbit to try and determine the source of the radio signals.

"The ship's sensor data had just started coming in indicating the emissions were coming from multiple points in the orbit and from the ground and the next thing I knew, there was a massive, blinding explosion off the left side of the ship and a second later—"

"What happened?"

"You want to hear the story or jump to the last page?" Adis barked.

Radnower remained silent and leaned back slightly.

Adis grumbled under his breath something about youth these days.

"Anyway, as I was saying, I passed out, and sometime later, I regained consciousness but that was more than I could say for my ship. She was mostly dead and in a slow tumble. I was able to reboot the emergency transponder, but couldn't functionally verify it because the ship was beginning to hit the upper parts of the atmosphere which increased the tumble rate of the ship, threatening to make me black out again—I was losing altitude fast. If I couldn't get some control back, I was going to burn up during re-entry. The landing part, I'd have to worry with that later.

Radnower made a sound under his breath while he extended one arm to rest on his knee, clenching it white knuckled. Tribal tattoos peaked out from under the jacket cuff, tickling some long-forgotten memory in Adis.

"Anyway, I couldn't establish power to the control thrusters, so I ripped out the power feed line from under the control panel and hot-wired it into the emergency computer power pack since it was the only system alive on the ship besides me. Things were happening fast, but a few sparks later, I got some intermittent control of the ship and pointed it in the right direction to survive the burn through the atmosphere.

"With the ship through the burning plasma, slowing, and relatively stable as it fell through the atmosphere, per my military training and working the most critical issue at a time, the next on the list was getting to the ground safely. There was nothing but water below me for as far as I could see to the horizon. Still, traveling around seven times the speed of sound, it wasn't long before I could see some land on the horizon. I used my attitude thrusters as best I could to continue slowing my descent with some hope of hitting it."

"Obviously, you landed safely," he said, slowly scanning the area.

"Long story short, I made it. Barely. In hindsight, I wonder if it'd have been better if I hadn't. Either way, I landed in what I later learned to be central Canada in the middle of nowhere. On my way down, I tried to send a distress signal home but I wasn't sure if it sent due to all the power I was diverting to the thrusters. Since no rescue's ever shown up, I guess that pretty much answers that question."

Radnower nodded slowly.

"I learned later that the explosion which disabled my ship was one of this planet's early orbital tests of nuclear weapons. As luck would have it, on July 9, 1962, the Starfish Prime test was launched from Johnston Island and detonated right next to my ship."

"That's before space program."

"I said I wasn't *from* this planet, boy! Anyway, the explosion caused a massive electro-magnetic pulse that my ship was not designed to withstand since we haven't used that technology on my planet for over a thousand years, so down I went. Hell, the explosion was so powerful it caused electrical damage in Hawaii, about 900 miles from the explosion."

Radnower's eyebrows raised slightly. "Surprising you survived."

"Good breeding, son. Plus a career as a military Space Force pilot.

"After a few days trekking through the damp alien forest, I finally made it to a town and tried to integrate into society as best I could. Fortunately, my image projection hardware had continued to function over the decades, which projects a 'human' form to the natives, allowing me to live and walk freely for the last half-century of this planet. However, in hindsight, I must have scared the hell out of that couple hiking in the forest that first day before I knew what the intelligent species—and I use that term loosely—looked like. Good ole Canadians, once they regained consciousnesses from the fright of seeing my natural form, they wished me good day and continued on." Adis let out a belly laugh which degraded into coughing spasms. Radnower stared with strained patience.

Adis regained his composure and continued. "Yeah, well, while the form projection technology makes me appear human while showing my representative age. And in the unlikely event you're in hostile territory for an extended period of time and aging is expected so as not to draw attention to yourself. Being away from my home world, I haven't had access to the needed microbiome to maintain my health and thus have aged significantly—more than normal. As it turns out, you humans live less than half as long as my people..." Adis' words trailed off as he got lost in memories from home.

After a few moments, Radnower cleared his throat.

"Oh yes, Scandinavian. I go by Eric Svenson now, since people thought my accent sounded Scandinavian. So, over the years, I made my way to New York. It's not the ideal place to be, but being around and watching you humans was better than living alone over the years. A few have tried to become friends with me, but while we could communicate just fine, as a species you're still very myopic. It's like trying to be friends with someone who only sees a foot or two of the ground around their feet and is oblivious to the universe around them. The conversation isn't exactly stimulating."

Radnower raised an eyebrow.

"But, you hold promise as a species, I suppose, if you can get your act together and make it through The Great Filter. Not many do, you know."

"Hmm. So, what did you do all of this time?" The young man showed some renewed interest.

Adis harrumphed. "I thought I'd better learn as much about the humans as I could before I was rescued because Central Command would want to know about this new species who were well on their way to space travel, at that time. Since your languages are fairly simple, I picked one up quickly and enrolled in one of the centers for higher learning. It was all very rudimentary and I might have even pointed them in the right direction in orbital mechanics and computational technology while studying as a graduate student...once the human space program got off the ground." Adis chuckled at the double meaning of the human words.

"Well, I guess I'm thinking like you now. Anyway, I went into engineering and eventually into the aerospace business sector. It had been a couple of decades since I crashed and decided I had best secure long-term provisions for myself in case a rescue party never arrived. Or at best, I could help sustain their rapid technology development with the hopes of being able to possibly gain the parts I needed to someday fix my ship.

"See, son, at that time, I was still in deep denial of the possibility of never being rescued. I couldn't come to terms with the fact I would always be marooned on an alien planet populated by a self-absorbed, troglodyte of a species. But because there was considerable momentum behind their space program, at least through the end of their twentieth century, I decided to help out a little here and there. In hallway conversations and low-level design meetings, I nudged them in the right direction in some orbital mathematics in the Mercury program. Later in the Apollo program, I might have helped them out with some of their early microcomputer hardware designs." Adis laughed, which spawned another series of coughs.

"I got them started out with some solar cell technology for their satellites and fuel pump technology for their Space Shuttle main engines. The way they were progressing, I hoped they might be well on their way to leaving your solar system by the time I grew too old. I would later learn of my folly on not anticipating your society losing interest in going into space, as well as the fact that I would age so much faster here. But I kept myself busy going from one company after another, mostly out of curiosity, but also it was better than dealing emotionally with the fact no one had come for me. No one. And they … never would."

Radnower shifted on the bench impatiently.

"The years passed very quickly and my body aged surprisingly fast, but I guess it was normal for you humans. I retired from the workforce. I have to tell you, these years since then have been the hardest. Living with a body that is wearing out, always in pain, and malfunctioning in new and creative ways every day. This is not how we do it on my world. We extend the life of a body to its extreme then let them pass before they are trapped in a failed body…"

Adis drifted away in thought for a few moments. "See, I told you I was a crazy old man." He cocked an eyebrow to gauge the young man's reaction.

No sooner had their gazes connected, Radnower barked, "What's your personal ID?"

"What?"

"I said, what's your personal ID, soldier?"

As if driven by instinct, his ancient body moved automatically, struggling to stand. Why, he wasn't sure, but he saluted, "CD-4295-12 Cartography, sir!"

Radnower gave a broad smile filled with years of fistfights and bad dentistry. "Yeah, you're a serious crazy old man. Good story, though. Guess you earned getting this over fast." He fluidly rose to his feet, face to face with Adis.

For the first time ever, Adis flinched. A cold shiver raced down his spine. It was hard to know if the chill reached is feet first or his sinking heart. It had actually felt really good to tell his story to someone who seemed like they at least cared enough to listen without obvious judgement. So it *was* going to happen. The punk was just entertaining himself before he took out his mark for the day. Perfect day for it, no one around. This was just all fun and games for him. *No! I changed my mind. I want to wait just a little longer. Don't do this!* But no words came; the cold, dry air had stolen his voice.

Radnower pushed up the arm of his jacket and extended it slowly toward him. Adis' eyes widened slightly in question.

What? What did he want? Push an old man down? I don't understand.

The young man's hand froze midway between them.

Did he want to shake hands? Don't be an old fool, Adis! You probably fell asleep on the bench and this is all another damn dream...

Oh, what the hell? No way to stand against the strength of youth...

He reciprocated.

No sooner had they grasped, the young man's tattoos faintly glowed blue and a rush of energy burst forth, energizing Adis' old body, causing every hair to stand on end and his skin to crawl with the sensation of ten thousand ants. His body collapsed back onto the bench, void of any remaining strength.

Arrrgg! What...what's going on...this quickening...?

123

When the pain-fueled tunnel vision finally subsided, Adis held up his phone and stared wide-eyed at the reflection on the surface...where a *new* young man now sat.

"What have you done?"

Radnower smiled gently. "Lieutenant Colonel Nothan, congratulations, you've verified your identity." His voice and accent had shifted slightly.

"I'm from the Lanthian Space Force. I'm here to take you home. Sorry it took us so long. I hope you're feeling a little better now. Unfortunately, I have to report that there's been trouble which delayed things, and we're once again in need of your service."

Off-World Kick Murder Squad VII

Daniel Arthur Smith

This is the seventh episode of the serialized novel Off-World Kick Murder Squad. Earlier episodes can be read in the previous Canyons issues

COULDA, WOULDA, SHOULDA...If we hadn't taken on those lizard birds, if we'd launched the *Jentu* directly after she was prepped, hell if we'd have taken to sky a mere few minutes earlier—we would've been clear. But we didn't. And now it looked like we weren't going anywhere upward anytime soon, pinned down by a column of syndicate troopers and a half dozen artillery mechs—just one of which, by the way, could put enough hurt on our delta wing to ensure we'd never fly again.

Hodge was matter of fact about it. "That's a whole lot of ugly," he said.

While Bailer was typical in his surety. "They're not going to fire. Not as long as the Indici is on board."

"You think?" asked Anson.

"You'll see. They'll be calling, any second."

And on cue, a series of clicks purred from the com.

"You're right," said Anson. "We have a call coming in." He spun clear so I could see the incoming signal on the com screen.

"Okay," I said. "Let's see what they have to say."

Anson tapped the com button and the signal on the screen was replaced with the face of a smug little man in a pristine white uniform. On his lapel he wore the insignia of a lieutenant, but his eyes weren't blue like ours; he wasn't a Bureau officer or a syn, which didn't surprise me in the slightest. He was one of the Korean syndicate's private army and for their own reasons, they stuck to a certain low-level breed of human. I'd seen his like too many times before. This guy had never known a battle and was itching to blast at something other than the local spry lizards. Guys like him rarely waste time getting to brass tacks and when he opened his mouth, he proved me right. "Let's make this quick," he said. "Give us back what you took, we'll pay your crew over and above whatever your fee is, and you can be on your way."

I played it coy. "I don't think I know what you're talking about."

"Sure you do. You're bounty hunters, and I'm offering a higher bounty. High as you like. Name your price."

"You have us confused with someone other than ourselves. We're not bounty hunters. We're barely in the people moving business."

Putting him on edge was easy, he was already triggered. "Don't play semantics with me," he said. "Someone hired you to deliver your cargo for a fee. It's the same thing. Now I don't care what line you're in. Your business is your business. I'm even willing to overlook the mess you made at the station. I'm just saying I'll offer you more. It's better for you and your crew all the way around. I'll give you a minute to think it over."

The screen went blank.

"Hmm," said Bailer.

"Hmm, what?" asked Hodge.

Bailer leaned into the windscreen for a tighter inspection. "He's going to take us out as soon as we hand Cerulean over."

"Agreed," I said.

Hodge shrugged. "But what if he means it?"

"Means what?" I asked.

"Well," said Hodge, "he's right. More is more. Maybe he's serious and if he is, why don't we just take what he's offering and then get on our way?'

I shook my head. "*If* he was serious—which he is not—but if he was, that would be too akin to bounty hunting, and we're not bounty hunters."

"But we—"

126

"No buts. I don't even like being confused with that sort. In fact, we go out of our way to avoid those folks on account that there's a bounty out there on our own heads and getting too close and mixing is bound to backfire eventually."

"I don't see how him calling us bounty hunters mixes us with them," said Hodge.

"It does."

"Well, then it ain't much difference. We took the lizard man against his will and we're delivering him for a fee. That's at least kidnapping."

"Okay," I said. "On this job, yes, we are still handing him over for a fee, but we freed him from a situation, and he was happy to come with us, not exactly kidnapping as I see it. I gave my word we'd deliver him safe and I'm sticking to it."

"But the syndicate man said he'd let us go."

Bailer grinned. "He was lying five ways."

"How you know?" asked Hodge.

"His biometrics were spiking. He certainly hasn't forgotten about our incursion, and notice how he wasn't interested in introductions?"

"I guess," said Hodge. "So what?"

"That means he's not planning on having us around long enough to bother learning our names."

Hodge touched his fingers to his temple. "Maybe that just means he wants to let us go."

I shook my head. "He ain't letting us go."

"Nine planes," said Hodge. Then he started with the questions. "Why can't anything be straight forward? What we going to do then?"

"Relax," I said.

"How much damage can they do with a single blast from one of those void cannons?"

Again, I said, "Relax."

This time, Hodge closed his mouth.

"Are you good?"

He nodded, so I went on. "The way I read the situation, the deal is his only play. We just need to play along. We position ourselves, make it like we're going to surrender, then when we have the chance, we make a run for it. Hodge, my brother, you find Lucinda and suit yourself up. I have a plan. But if they don't go for it, we'll need to be blazing."

Hodge gave me a tooth filled grin then stepped past me to exit the bridge. "Excuse me," I heard him say then turned to find Sss'karo at the door.

I smiled at the reptoid. "Seems we weren't quite as evasive as I'd thought."

His slender tongue flicked out of his closed mouth then back. From what I've read of reptiles, he was smelling the room. He repeated the flick, then said, "I heard what you sss'aid Caw-aptain. About keeping your word."

"Don't get too sentimental. We got a job, we gotta make good."

He replied with a drop of his head to the side. Maybe he was just getting a look at me from a different angle or maybe it meant nothing at all, but I determined he was reading me for truth—which compelled me to add, "They're not going to let us leave either way. We might as well take you with us." That seemed to affect him because his head went straight again.

And it was timely, because right then the com started to purr.

I gave Anson the nod and the lieutenant came back on the screen.

He was quick to it. "Are you ready to reason?" he asked.

"Sure," I said. "But we have some conditions."

"Just take a glance out your window, we have the high ground. There will be no conditions. I already told you to name your price. Give me a number, hand over your cargo, and you can be on your way."

"You're right, you do have the upper hand, and that makes me uneasy. I mean, Sol System or not, this hidden planet might as well be a backwater. How do we know you'll let us go once we hand him over?"

"Don't wear my patience. Just give me—" The lieutenant stopped speaking. He began to twitch and blink. His face flushed with confusion. But it wasn't our discussion that seemed to be irritating him. If I'd have guessed, he was making the face of a man with a thousand voices screaming in his head.

Little did I know at that second how right I was.

While this was happening, our bridge took on an ominous indigo glow.

"What's going on?" asked Anson. "Why's he—"

"It's Sss'karo," I said softly. The Indici was standing beside me, out of sight of the lieutenant. The reptoid was still as a statue, facing forward in somewhat of a trance. But as still as his body was, the furnace fueling those blue flames where his eyes should have been burned brilliantly.

I looked to the reptoid, to the screen, then back again. I had no clue how he was managing it.

On the screen, the lieutenant continued his fight to resist, his cheeks creased deep and his nose scrunched up tight. A gurgle escaped him, then an, "Arrrrnnnooooo!" Then his brow hardened, and his eyes took on a menacing stare. And though they were two different creatures entirely—the lieutenant and the Indici—they appeared to mirror each other.

I've been to many a battle, seen mayhem and slaughter, but what I saw happen up on that ridge was particularly heinous.

There were six Mechs spread across the long crest of that hill. The mech farthest to the right—the one I figure was piloted by the lieutenant—spun its long dual barrels toward the middle of the group. Then immediately, a pulsed torrent of red flame shot out of the cannons, obliterating the second and third mechs in the line and sending a vibrating concussion through the *Jentu*. The syndicate troopers lined up beneath the mechs—those who weren't immediately incinerated—scrambled from the flames, then they too, began to fire upon each other. Then the mech to the far left swung its guns toward the line and let loose its artillery.

The screen went blank—and it was over.

There was a pinch in my craw, and my words were dry. "Let's not wait," I said. "Get us high."

Anson ignited the engines and the *Jentu* took lift, leaving the remnants of fire fight below.

Once we were aloft, Sss'karo's blue fire dulled to its previous glow, and with twitch of his own, he came back to life. "They will not pursssue," he said.

We said nothing.

"I'll be returning to my caw-abin," he added.

I could only nod.

As he exited the bridge, Hodge entered again, a helmet on his head and an armor plate on his chest. He was holding the rail with one hand and Lucinda in the other.

"What the nine planes happened?" he said. "Were they firing on us? How'd we get up?"

What had just happened wasn't sitting well with any of us who witnessed it, so there was nothing said.

"What?" asked Hodge, his eyes darting from face to face.

Then Bailer cleared his throat. "Hrrm," he said. "Sss'karo took care of it."

"So, we're on our way to the Martian rendezvous?"

"I gave my word," I said.

"Good thing you did too," said Anson. "I think Sss'karo was impressed."

"He was," I agreed. "But when I said I gave my word, I meant my word to Slayden, not Sss'karo. If we cross Slayden, we'll have a world of troubles coming our way."

"Based on what we witnessed," said Bailer, "we have a world of troubles coming our way regardless."

In earnest, I'll tell you that as good as it was to be planet side, it was all the better to be back in the black and on our way to the rendezvous. It was just Anson, Bailer, and myself who saw what had happened up on that ridge, and I asked them to keep it to themselves. They were happy to oblige. That in itself is something that only happens on rare occasion. Anson is always on board but, as I mentioned before, Bailer likes to test rope. As it were, none of them wanted to replay the day, so getting them not to say so much wasn't all that hard. Don't get me wrong, we're tagged a kick murder squad for a reason; if killing needs to be done, then it's done. But despite our reputation, we were once military ourselves and though it may be that neither humans nor the syndicate are at the top of our lists, not a one of us cared to see those soldiers so effortlessly massacred.

What was even more troublesome is that it didn't seem to bother Sss'karo in the least. I mean, the Indici physiology isn't partial to an exhibit of feelings per se, so his matter of fact way of destruction only served to creep me and the boys out further than we'd already been. Made me question myself as to whether we'd made the right choice keeping him on board. Thankfully, Cassidy, Rhia, and Rhoe hadn't a clue as to how it went down, and as far as Hodge, he thought we just made a clean break and escaped fire, which I surely appreciated on all parts. Not so much Cassidy and the twins, they themselves are far more pragmatic than I'm comfortable with at times. But Hodge, for a such a tough, is actually quite delicate. I mean, I can't imagine what he would do with knowing Sss'karo was able mind bend like that, and if I tried to imagine I don't suppose I'd like what I'd see.

We did have some luck, though; there was no sign of pursuit. There was no one left on that ridge to report us, and if a message had gotten out from the station, it happened after we were gone. The way I figure, it's never good for a security detail to report that they failed at their sole mission, so my guess is that they wanted to keep the heist local and resolve it themselves. Besides that, it wasn't like they could send a signal direct from a hidden planet. Any communication had to be personally delivered through the Bubble, and I'm sure who ever had that honor went in only after they'd lost contact with the mechs.

Anyway, we left free and clear without anyone on our trail, and once we cleared orbit, that entire planet simply disappeared in its shimmer, like it'd never been at all.

There was just us, back in the black, Mars-bound, with a guest. And let it be said that the squad is resilient. As it was, the shadow of the day, if there was one, didn't loom. Wasn't too long before everyone settled into a routine and things were back to as normal as they could get—well, not everything. One thing we couldn't shake was Will laid out in the infirmary. The crew took turns keeping vigil, which was about all we could do. And then there was the full hold of lizard birds to contend with. Hodge took them on as a personal project. They were quiet and peaceful like, but they smelled something awful when we brought them on, and the odor worsened by the day. Every morning, Hodge put on a space suit and took up the air hose. He pressure-washed the mess off the floor of the hold and into the airlock, pulled the atmosphere back, then mopped up the deck, all while being particularly careful of his feathered friends. It didn't eliminate the smell of the birds themselves, but we were better off less the bio-waste.

And Sss'karo, he settled in too, started mingling with the crew and having dinner with us. Rhia and Rhoe prepared the vegetables they'd gathered. Hodge took several stabs at cooking the frozen lizard bird. Turns out the Indici are vegetarian. Cassidy took a particular liking to him, answering his questions, showing him how things were done. I'm not sure if he was interested because we were syns or because, to him, we were close to being mortals, or maybe he just sensed that Cassidy was nonjudging. Of course, Cassidy has a way with everyone. You could say she was built for it. And Cassidy being friendly with the Indici led the others to ease. Rhia and Rhoe taught him to play dice, Anson talked to him about engineering. If you pushed me, I'd say that even I began to find him a little less creepy.

Things took a change about a week into flight. It was late, some had gone to quarters, and I decided to take the time to sit in the infirmary with Will. A few nights before, I'd seen Bailer in there reading aloud to Will a story from the Archive. I asked him why he was doing that, and he had told me that it was something he used to do with the infirmed soldiers—mortals and syns alike. He said if there was one thing humans and syns had in common, it was that there was a good chance their minds were still working even if their bodies weren't. Reading aloud, talking to them, any interaction helped the healing process. Fascinated by the idea, I'd loaded my digital pad with some poetry.

I'm not sure if it helped Will at all, reading the stanzas aloud, but it certainly helped me. We'd done everything we could do for him—cleaned, patched him, connected everything we had onboard that could help keep him functioning. And it wasn't that he didn't look peaceful, he did—as much as he could with all of that equipment bound to him—but there was a helplessness I held for myself, not knowing if he was living or dying or both.

I suppose I'd been reading for quite some time when Cassidy and Sss'karo appeared at the door.

"Hey Cass, Sss'karo," I said, putting the digital on my lap.

Cassidy had a calmness about her. "That's nice," she said. "I didn't know you were into the works of Drahan."

"I took a liking to him during the war. There was a sergeant I served with on the fields of Kalanthia, used to recite him late at night, made it all just a bit bearable."

"Was Will that sergeant?"

"He was. Now what can I do you for?"

It was Sss'karo who answered. "It'sss what I may be able to do for you, Caw-aptain."

"On with it," I said. "Don't make me guess."

"Sss'karo has been concerned about the crew," said Cassidy. "He's sensed we've been upset. About Will. He says he thinks he can help."

"Has he now?" I said. "I thought your particular skills didn't work on synthetics like ourselves."

132

"You are caw-rrect," said Sss'karo. "But anyone can sssurely notissse that your caw-rew isss out of harmony."

"I see. I didn't realize we were wearing it on our sleeves."

"Thisss isss him?" Sss'karo entered the infirmary. "Your injured medic?"

"Yes," I said.

As he approached the med bed, his thin tongue slithered in and out, smelling the room. When he reached Will, he rotated his head, the way I'd become accustomed to seeing, further analyzing our fallen comrade. "He isss an important member of your caw-rew. Yes?"

"Yeah," I said.

"More than that," said Cassidy.

I nodded. "Cass speaks true. He's part of our family, he's our friend."

"What happened to him?" he asked.

"He was shot," Cassidy said. "Then his eyes went dim." She gestured to the screens at the head of the med bed and the lines that led to electrodes pasted to Will's temples, chest, and arms. "We aren't able to get a strong reading from his neural lace. Will is our medic and—other than keep his body alive with all these machines—we're at a loss as to what we can do."

"His eyes are dim," said Sss'karo, "but they are not out. I may be able to help." His head snapped toward me. "With your permission, of courssse."

"Surely," I said. "If you think you can help, then by all means."

Sss'karo laid his blue scaled hand across Will's forehead and to my astonishment, Will's eyes opened, lit bright, then they went dim again.

Under my breath, I whispered, "Nine planes."

"He is in there," said Sss'karo.

"Apparently so."

"But hisss body needsss more telinium to feed the repair nanosss."

"We gave him all the telinium we had, we just didn't happen to have much on hand."

"He will not lassst much longer in thisss ssstate." He shifted is hand then, talons spread wide, placed his other above the compression wrap on Will's chest. "I'm sssurprisssed that he lasssted thisss long. Thisss body can be repaired but in doing so, there isss a high-risk your friend will die."

Upon hearing this, Cassidy took Will's hand into her own. "Is there nothing we can do?" she asked.

"Sssince the neural lassse isss intact, hisss conssscience ssshould be removed, then the body can be repaired without risssk."

"That would be great," said Cassidy. "But again, we weren't able to get a strong reading on his neural lace. Not enough for a transfer anyway."

"There isss another way," said Sss'karo. "I can transfer his caw-onscience into myssself, though there is a caw-aveat. Once inside, we would not be able to transssfer through a lassse interfassse. He would have to ssstay in my ssshell until either hisss body isss ready, or I am in physssical caw-ontact with another vesssel with neural lassse."

"Well," I said. "If it's the only way to save Will, you should do it."

"Should we check with the others?" asked Cassidy.

"Do you think it will change things?" I asked.

"No," she said.

"Then I say we let him do his best." I gave Sss'karo a nod, he nodded back, then placed his hand on Will again, and again Will's eyes flared bright blue, then went out.

Cassidy and I set Sss'karo up on the other med bed and connected him to Will in the way he asked. By the time we finished, there was web of cables and machines between them. Of course, when the crew roused the next morning, they took notice, and when I entered the galley, they were already gathered and waiting for me to explain.

So I did. And after sharing with them exactly what had transpired, I closed with, "That's how it is and how it's going to be."

Bailer was the first to speak. "So it's only temporary?" he asked.

"It is," said Cassidy. "As soon as Will's body is healed, Sss'karo will put him back."

"Because we do have a rendezvous to deliver that Indici, and you said yourself, Cap, if we cross Slayden, we'll have a world of troubles coming our way."

"We just need more telinium to speed up the process," said Cassidy. "Then we can turn him over."

"And I'm confident," I added, "that we can get all the telinium we need once we reach Mars."

"Telinium is a miracle drug for syns but not much use to humans," said Rhia.

"True," I said.

"Well, haven't most of the colonial syns been moved further off-world?"

"There are only a few syn mortals left on Mars," said Anson. "But a lot of syn livestock. They'll have plenty telinium in their stores to keep them healthy."

I nodded. "That's how I figure, and being we're going in as livestock traders, we should be able to get our hands on what we need without too much trouble. In the meantime, we'll all need to give blood—plasma anyway."

"Sure," said Hodge, "I'll give Will all I got, but how will that help?"

"Sss'karo says our blood contains enough telinium to keep Will's body on the mend."

"Really?" asked Hodge. "We got enough telinium coursing through our veins to help him out?" He sniffed his forearm. "Sounds off to me."

"Even the trace amounts help," said Cassidy. "It's not enough to heal him full, but enough to pull him through until we get more."

Not a one of the others looked convinced.

"I'm not going to lie," I said, "I know it sounds off. But there was a chance to save Will and I took it."

Bailer poked in again. "Cassidy," he said, "is that how you saw it?"

"I brought Sss'karo to the Captain," she said. "I believe he can help him."

"That's good enough for me," he said.

It rubbed me wrong that my word wasn't good enough, but I let it slide. Mostly 'cuz I had to tend to Hodge.

"It's not good enough for me," said Hodge. "That lizard's lying in there, his eyes wide open, wires going from his head to Will's. It's just creepy. And how does this even work without a lace interface?"

"Well," I said, "for one, Sss'karo's eyes aren't wide open. He doesn't seem to have eyelids. It is a bit creepy, but he's dormant right now, and I suppose that's helping. And as far as a lace interface, Sss'karo doesn't seem to need one. That's the entirety of him helping out. My guess is he set aside a space in his brain for Will—and they're sharing it." I shrugged. "I don't rightly understand it."

"There wouldn't be enough space," said Hodge. "Everyone knows lizards got small brains."

Bailer grinned. "Works for you, big guy."

135

Hodge smirked. "Captain said we ain't from lizards."

I rolled an eye at Bailer. "I'm sure his brain pan is right fitted."

"Uh huh," said Hodge. "And how do we know he's not faking it just so we don't turn him in when the time comes?"

Cassidy shook her head. "He's not."

"But how do you know?"

"I know," she said. "It's hard to explain. But you had to see what we saw."

We were about a day out from Mars—our last night in the black—and I was taking my turn with my fallen friend. We'd already been taking our turns sitting with Will, but we set up an orderly rotation to regulate the transfusions. With all of the swabbing going on, the infirmary had taken on that strong disinfectant odor of rubbing alcohol you'd expect it sometimes does. Even with the *Jentu's* air circulation, the vapors hung still in the room, coated my eyes and tongue. I had a needle in one arm and held a digital pad in the other. And I was reading Drahan again— just seemed fit for the time. Psychology is a funny thing because, even though Will's conscience was in the Indici behind me, I was reading to Will's body and to be true, I figured it didn't matter which direction I was in. I was, though, a lot more convinced about it helping than when I'd started a week before. The telinium in our blood, as trace as it was, was definitely making a difference because, according to the diagnostics, the hole in Will's chest, as gaping as it had been, was visibly pulling together. And though I know better, Will's recovery had me thinking nostalgic. It was when I read the line, '*the waves roll in, the waves roll out*', that I took pause from the poetry to let Will in. "You know," I said aloud. "I may not understand just what it is the Indici is doing, but once I explained best I could to the squad, they were all in—even Rhia and Rhoe, small as they are, are giving what plasma they can to put you on the mend. Heh, but you and me, this isn't the first time we've traded blood is it? Between blaster wounds, saber cuts and what all, I seem to remember a span we spent all of our downtime in the infirmary, a line in the vein."

You know there's a misconception that syns don't exhibit emotions. That couldn't be further from the truth. We're like humans in most every way, more than we care to admit. We're just turned up a few more notches on the dial—and that means the ability to control those emotions too. So, contrary to another myth—that syns don't cry—

right at that moment, talking to my brother on the table, my eyes had gone misty.

"You know what else?" I continued. "I thought you were done. The way your eyes went out. I mean, how many times did we see eyes go dim? Potter, Welsh, Bob, Freddy—I could go on and on, a dozen syns in one day on Kalanthia. So many syn soldiers, their eyes dimmed and they never came back. Now, of course, I'm sitting here wondering if those soldiers could have been saved too. Imagine that. It's a thought that's never come to me before. There's been other thoughts about the off-world conflicts. Thoughts about syns killing syns, that we were toy soldiers for the syndicate and the bureau alike–there were those thoughts. There were the thoughts that drew us, me and you, our whole band, together. But never did I ponder that spark of life we possess was any less as potent or fragile as any human's or the fact that without that spark, we're mere bags of meat. Like the poet says, 'The waves roll in and the waves roll out'."

Maybe the regular loss of blood plasma was making me light headed, or maybe it was the lateness of the hour, but with those words spent, a stillness followed, washed over the room, making the subtle purr of the transfuser and the interment chirp of the med bed deafening. I inhaled deeply and resettled myself in the chair; the needle slightly pinched as I shifted.

Then I went back to the digital pad and took up reading aloud where I'd left off, "The waves roll in, the—"

"The wavesss roll out." Sss'karo interrupted. "Damn, Ellsss. How many timesss you going to repeat it? The wavesss roll in, the wavesss roll out, the wavesss roll in, the wavesss roll out."

Except is didn't sound like Sss'karo. I mean it did, and it was, but when I looked at him, he seemed different. The Indici's speech was not as slow as before and he was physically more animate than his usual stiff self. His long-clawed fingers ran up his body and across the scalp, a tactile inspection of the wires and electrodes connecting him to the machines and back to Will.

"That was a clossse one," he said. "I thought they had me there."

"They?" I asked.

"Thossse Bureau Boysss behind me. Why do I sssound so ssstrange. Iss something on my—" His slender tongue slipped out and back, causing him to shake his head in a quiver. "What wasss that?"

"Will?" I asked. "Is that you?"

137

"Who elssse would it be, Ells?" His tongue shot out and back again. "I don't feel quite like myssself."

ABOUT THE AUTHORS

Gustavo Bondoni is an Argentine writer with over a hundred stories published in fourteen countries, in seven languages, and is a winner in the **National Space Society's "Return to Luna" Contest** and the **Marooned Award for Flash Fiction** (2008). His fiction has appeared in the **Texas STAAR English Test cycle, The Rose & Thorn, Albedo One, The Best of Every Day Fiction** and many others.

His latest books are a comic fantasy romp: **The Malakiad** (2018) and a military SF adventure, **Incursion** (2017). He has also published two science fiction novels: **Outside** (2017) and **Siege** (2016). He has also recently published an ebook novella entitled **Branch**. His previously published short fiction is collected in **Tenth Orbit and Other Faraway Places** (2010) and **Virtuoso and Other Stories** (2011). **The Curse of El Bastardo** (2010) is a short fantasy novel.

M. M. De Voe writes interstitial fiction and has been published in magazines ranging from the **St. Petersburg Review** to **Daily Science Fiction**. Her poetry has won first place in the **Lyric** as well as the **NYC's PoetTweet** contest. She has also won top prizes in flash fiction, literary fiction and horror, and co-wrote a sci-fi musical that was produced by Tisch School of the Arts. Founder of the literary nonprofit **Pen Parentis**, she lives in Manhattan, writes what she likes, and does the next thing on a daily basis.

Ann Stolinsky is the founder and owner of Gontza Games, an independent board and card game company.
Several of her stories have been published in the last few years.

Molly Thynes has been everything from a student at an all-girl's Catholic school to a nanny, a purveyor of haunted artifacts, and a mental health counselor, but she has been a writer before she even knew how to write. Her first love is the horror genre but she has found inspiration in a few other genres too (just not romance). Currently, Molly lives in Saint Paul, MN with her husband and as many animals as their landlord will allow.

Barry Charman is a starving writer of oddball stories. Published in **Ambit, Popshot, The Alarmist, Bare Fiction Magazine** & **Firewords Quarterly**.

Jason LaVelle is an author, photographer, and podcaster from West Michigan. When he's not spending time with his beautiful wife and four children, LaVelle works at a veterinary clinic, helping animals of all kinds. With his two pugs, Dragon and Mr. Sparkles, his Chihuahua, Mari, and his annoying dachshund, Lady, LaVelle pretty much lives in a zoo. After he's done playing with the pugs and tucking the kids into bed, LaVelle ventures down into the basement, where his umbrella cockatoo, Bella whispers in his ear like a demonic muse, forcing him to explore the paranormal world inside his mind.

Nathan M. Beauchamp started writing stories at nine years old and never stopped. From his first grisly tales about carnivorous catfish, mole detectives, and cyborg housecats, his interests have always delved into strange waters. Nathan works in finance so that he can support his habit of putting words together in the hope that someone will read them. His hobbies include reading, photography, arguing for sport, and pondering the eventual heat death of the universe. He has published many short stories in magazines and anthologies and holds an MFA in creative writing from Western State. He lives in Colorado with his wife and two young boys. Nathan co-created the award winning YA science fiction series **Universe Eventual** where he writes as N.J. Tanger. The series includes **Chimera, Helios,** and **Ceres** and the prequel **Ascension. Universe Eventual** is available on Amazon.

Charles Barouch's quest to never stop learning has made him a fiction author, a journalist, a teacher, and a technologist. You can find some of his other fiction writings on Amazon, Nook, and Kobo. His current journalism is in the pages of International Spectrum. You can hear him speak at Otakon and Spectrum Conferences.
And, he's been known to hang out on social media platforms if you'd like to talk.

Terry R. Hill, a Texas native, was trained with two degrees in aerospace engineering. He has worked for NASA since 1997 with a very satisfying career as an engineer and project manager spanning programs from the international space station's navigation software, to next generation space suit design, to exploration mission planning, to mitigating the health effects of space on astronauts. While supporting the manned space program has been a lifetime passion, writing of different worlds, alternate futures and the human condition has filled his spare time.

Jessica West (a.k.a. West1Jess) is currently pursuing a state of self-induced psychosis, also known as writing. In the past, she has worked for Wal-Mart, a lawyer, and a bank. Now if she could just get a couple years experience with the IRS and the NSA, world domination is in the bag.

Jess lives in Acadiana with three daughters still young enough to think she's cool and a husband who knows better but likes her anyway.

For more information, visit west1jess.com.

Daniel Arthur Smith is a USA Today bestselling author. His titles include ***Spectral Shift, Hugh Howey Lives, The Cathari Treasure, The Somali Deception***, and a few other novels and short stories. He also curates the phenomenal short fiction series ***Tales from the Canyons of the Damned*** and ***Frontiers of Speculative Fiction***.

He was raised in Michigan and graduated from Western Michigan University where he studied philosophy, with focus on cognitive science, meta-physics, and comparative religion. He began his career as a bartender, barista, poetry house proprietor, teacher, and then became a technologist and futurist for the Fortune 100 across the Americas and Europe.

Daniel has traveled to over 300 cities in 22 countries, residing in Los Angeles, Kalamazoo, Prague, Crete, and now writes in Manhattan where he lives with his wife and young sons.

For more information, visit danielarthursmith.com

www.ingramcontent.com/pod-product-compliance
Lightning Source LLC
Chambersburg PA
CBHW021918170626
46807CB00007B/2882